The Origin of Doubt

The Origin of Doubt

Fifty Short Fictions

Nathan Alling Long

Press 53
Winston-Salem

Press 53, LLC
PO Box 30314
Winston-Salem, NC 27130

First Edition

Cover design by Tiffany Ruiz

Author photo by Gary Plouff

Library of Congress Control Number: 2017964653

Printed on acid-free paper
ISBN 978-1-941209-73-8

To those who don't quite fit in

Grateful thanks to the editors of the publications where these stories first appeared:

5x5, "A House Divided"
52/250, "Alignment"
Amoskeag, "Abandoned"
Atticus Review, "Voice Lessons"
Brilliant Flash Fiction, "A Future Story"
Cadavre Exquis (anthology, Medusa's Laugh Press), "Another Story"
Camera Obscura, "Buried"
Clackamas Literary Review, "In the Palm of Your Hand"
College Hill Review, "Billy Tipton Day"
Dispatch Literary Journal, "In China"
Driftwood, "Half Your Age and Twice as Wise"
Failbetter, "The Devil"
Flash Fiction Press, "This Was My Plan"
Friends Journal, "Holy Days"
Fringe, "Jealousy"
I-70 Review, "The State We're In"
Ilannot Review, "Portraits of a Woman"
Indiana Review, "Them"
JMWW, "You Who I've Cornered"
Jonathan, "Crepuscular" and "Current"
Journal for Compressed Arts, "That Long Evening on Our Balcony"
Marco Polo Arts Magazine, "Genre" and "Keeping Us at Bay"
Monkeybicycle, "Flies"
Per Contra, "Contemporary"
The Portland Review, "Lindsey and I"
Salt Hill, "Christmas" and "The Origin of Doubt"
Seek It: Writers and Artists Do Sleep (anthology, Red Claw Press), "The Scent of Light"
See the Elephant, "Without a Rope"
Sequestrum, "How to Bury Your Dog"
Silk Road, "Sweeping"
Stripped (anthology, PS Press), "Breaking Tradition"

Story Quarterly, "Between"

Turn: A Season of Short-Short Stories (anthology, ELJ
    Publications, "The Ambassador")

TQ Review, "When the Moon Closes Its Eye"

Tusculum Review, "Chicken," "Fireflies," and "Sentries"

Two Hawks Review, "When My Mother Died"

WhiskeyPaper, "Ice Cream Truck," "Liana," and "The
    Fortunate"

Whispering Campaign, "Taro"

Wigleaf, "A Box of Things"

Wilde Magazine, "Fortune" and "Reconstruction"

Contents

I.

The Origin of Doubt

The Scent of Light

The last time he was taken to the hospital, after that long year of visits, he was placed on a table which slid into a giant white metal machine. The machine closed in around him and groaned so that it made him see blue light. But he wasn't afraid. He simply imagined he was Mickey from *The Night Kitchen*, falling through the pitcher of milk, then sitting in his pan of batter in the oven. He'd been told not to move his head, so he lay still, tracing his finger along the bleached white sheet on which he lay, imagining the yeasty scent of bread rising off his taut, pale skin.

"You okay in there?" asked the woman outside the machine. "We've got another ten minutes."

He understood her words, though they felt funny, like tiny paper rocks. He imagined her the baker, her plain green clothes smelling of flour and milk. He said nothing, because he was Mickey, and no one was to know he was in the loaf pan, hidden in the batter.

The room outside the machine had been upsetting. When he had first entered, he covered his ears against the loud noises falling from the ceiling. His mother had warned him not to be scared. But now, it was not hard to lie patiently in the confines of these quiet round walls.

After the machine stopped its soft whirl and it slid him out, he remained still, even as the taste of the room's colors—the yellow walls, the woman's green clothes, the red and white sign above the door—agitated him. Then he bolted up, raising his hands as if they were bursting through a crust. He shouted above the sound of the lights, "Surprise! Surprise!"

The woman in green smiled and said he was the best patient she'd ever had. He sat there, rolling each of her words in his small hands like they were ever-shrinking marbles—until there was nothing left to play with but dust in his palms.

Later, under the tree that sang in their backyard, his mother held him in her lap, the heat of her body a lavender scent radiating all around him. He could not look her in the face, with the water trickling from her eyes—each drop prickling the skin of his fingers like thistles. "How do I tell you this?" she said. Her words were unlike any that had come from her before: lonely chunks of metal, pockmarked, with jagged edges around the rim. He did not want to pick them up or touch them, but out of her mouth they came, like boulders falling onto his stomach and chest and head. Only the lavender of her heat could dissolve them.

"There's something in your brain, munchkin," she said, the sassafras leaves above them still singing their chirpy song. "And no one seems to know how to get it out."

As she talked, he saw how the words themselves were only tiny black seeds; it was the tone of her voice that encased each in a heavy metallic shell. He wished that they were lighter, like the pebbles of bird songs, but nothing seemed to make them shrink. So he lifted his small hands to her face and covered her lips with his fingers.

That night as he lay in bed, he listened to her read his favorite books. Afterwards, how could he sleep, with all the colors from those stories swarming above him like butterflies?

She sat there silent, then said dark-seeded words again, now in a calmer, more porcelain voice. "I don't want to lose you. I don't even know how to." He nodded as he let the small gray balls of her syllables roll off the blankets and disappear beneath his bed. When she brushed his hair in long, slow strokes, he thought of fresh baked bread.

"We'll have to start by practicing saying goodbye," she finally said. It was a long black snake of a sentence that seemed to slip into his ear and crawl down his throat, as though it would replace his spine. He reached out his hand and touched the fur of his yellow giraffe, a sweet taste that always gave him comfort. Yet that could not make the snake completely disappear. He looked up at the ceiling then; the colors from the storybooks had all withdrawn.

She looked at him for a long time, then leaned in close and kissed his forehead—and he was suddenly in a garden of flowers. He held on to the scent for as long as he could. And when the last of the petals had dropped away, she was gone—but so too was the snake in his body. He looked around his room then, softly touching the outline of everything, the buttery light of the moon coming in through the celery-like window.

"Goodbye chair," he said, practicing. "Goodbye desk." He felt the familiar edges of each object with his eyes. "Goodbye lamp. Goodbye books." He was now the rabbit of the story, growing sleepy in the velvety dark. "Goodbye giraffe, goodbye lemony sheets."

He finished circling the room and said, "Goodbye window, goodbye night." Then he closed his eyes, though he could still smell the light that came into the room.

"Goodbye earth," he said. "Goodbye moon."

Between

For ten smoky, stainless-steel minutes once a month I got to talk to my father. The minutes started out deadly long, like a session under a dentist's drill, then seemed to end as quick as breath: the two blue-clothed guards taking him away, the man who had just convinced me, one more time, to call him Dad.

Before the next month was up, I would forget his face, forget almost that he was really my father.

What I always remembered, though, were the three vertical metal bars that ran from the ceiling to the counter between us. They were painted with a thick gray paint, nicked and flaking.

From where I sat, Dad's face fit just between the outer two bars, with one single bar between, so that if I wanted to look at both of his eyes, he had no nose, and if I wanted to see his nose, he lost one eye. No matter how long I sat there looking at him, there was always something missing.

I was young—seven, then eight, then nine, then ten— and I barely knew what to say to him, how to tell him about my life in less time than it took for Mom and I to drive out to that place from home.

Once, to end an uncomfortable silence, I asked him why he was called a convict. I'd heard two kids say the word on the playground the week before, and I knew they were talking about my father.

"You know why they call us that, don't you?" he said, his eyes shiny beneath his yellowed skin. "They call us that 'cause we have convictions," he said.

Dad's voice was naturally deep, gravelly, but he tried to smile it up for me, so it was never quite serious, never quite his own. I didn't know whether to believe him or not. I looked at both his eyes, then shifted in my seat and looked at the center of his face. His left eye disappeared, then his right.

"*We* believe in something," he said in his half-raised voice. The guards appeared at his chair then, about to take him away. He stood up, as straight as he could.

"I believe," he said, then he disappeared.

The Devil

The boy was cast as the devil in a third-grade play. His outfit was a red union suit and his makeup, red food dye and Vaseline. He carried a curtain rod his mother had taken from his father's room, spray-painted Rustoleum red, with the tip of an old meat carving fork—which his father had never used—wedged into the top. For his forked tail, she had cut the red power cord to his father's electric mower—his father who no longer lived with them. His mother now hired a high-school kid, who used his own gas mower to cut the lawn, and to do everything his father once did.

The boy was a devil for only one night, but he did not like the thought of it, as though some evil might get under his skin. So, he was relieved that his mother had missed the performance. And after the play, when a neighbor dropped him off at his house, he went straight into the bathroom, washed his face, then threw the costume in the trash. But as he was brushing his teeth, the clothes and staff seemed to rustle in the can. So, he sealed them in a bag and took it out, walking carefully along the red brick path to the trashcans in the alley way.

He let the bag fall to the bottom of the can, as if it were a deep, deep well. And as he shut the metal lid, he felt as though there were eyes that watched him. The night was dark, the alley bare. He peered in all directions until he saw what he saw, through his mother's bedroom glass. The two-headed beast.

He raced back to the house, his small white feet running over the newly mowed lawn. The hair-like cuttings clung to the bottom of his feet; the cold wet grass felt like tiny snakes.

The Ambassador

My sister Frieda and I are in the tub. The water gives off a sad metal smell which I like. It will disappear when our mom comes in and makes us use the soap. But for now, we are in a boat in the ocean, and the ocean is also in a boat. The day is overcast—it is about to rain. That's the way the bathroom always feels under the sky light. We're taking a bath this morning because Mom was too busy with the party last night to give us one.

Frieda is bunching the edges of the washcloth, sinking it underwater to make an air balloon, then squeezing it so that it farts underwater and bubbles up. I'm watching over her.

I hear the washing machine running in the basement and my father cough at the dining room table, as he does every morning. I smell his cigarette smoke seep up the stairs. It is too strong and sour, like Brussels sprouts. We live Washington, D.C., and my father works for the government.

Frieda says, "Watch this, watch this!" but I'm listening for the doorbell—not that anyone will come by, but a visit is an event, and I like events. Last night was an event, a big cocktail party which mother said we had to be extra good for. *No coming down stairs. There's going to be an ambassador.*

And there was. I stayed in my room, but couldn't sleep with all the voices downstairs. I was still awake when he came up for his coat and stopped by my bedroom door and said hello. He must have seen my light on.

I didn't know him but I wasn't afraid. I said, "You can come in, but we have to whisper because Frieda is sleeping next door."

He sat in the chair next to the bed and asked me, "Why are you awake so late?"

"Too much noise downstairs," I said.

He laughed and apologized.

"It's okay," I said. I asked him what he did, as a job.

"I'm an ambassador," he said.

Then he told me that he had traveled around the world.

"What's the strangest thing you've ever seen?" I asked.

"Once I saw a man riding an elephant," he said. "He was feeding it hay that the elephant was carrying on its back. For some reason it struck me as funny."

I smiled. It was a funny thing to imagine.

We talked for a half hour, about trains, and the distance to the sun, about what an ambassador does and how many countries there are in the world.

There's so much I still need to see, even though I'm already seven.

Before he left, he said, "I've liked our chat. I think you are very bright." I've been holding on to that all morning. I won't tell anyone about it, so that it will be completely mine.

Now it's just Frieda and me in the tub, and I want something else to happen. After we bathe, we will eat. Everything is backwards from how we do it at night, which sort of makes it an event.

I look at Frieda, who is still squeezing washcloth balloons under water. She never gets the last bit of air and I have to help her, though she doesn't like it. She's small and needs help. She's old enough to talk, but not to ambassadors.

I watch her, wishing at least the phone would ring. Maybe he would call, wanting to talk to me, or maybe it would be someone else, telling us we have won a trip around the world.

Frieda has now laid the washcloth out flat, like a raft, and is placing her plastic animals on the surface. But the washcloth sinks before she can get them all on.

Downstairs, Dad coughs and mumbles something to Mom. The washing machine has stopped and she talks back from another room. Her voice is even more muffled and unclear. My father's smoke makes me think our house is on fire.

Mom will be up soon to check on us, to make us use soap. I listen hard for the phone or the doorbell, but there is nothing.

I look at Frieda's washcloth raft, which has fallen underwater again. I smell the smoke from distant fires. I remember then that we are on a boat at sea. *We need to escape*, I tell her.

We are going to a distant land, where men ride hippos and monkeys ride bicycles, and fish can swim on land. I imagine being the first one to discover this place. I imagine putting a flag on the ground and calling it mine. I'll be the first ambassador. But we have to find that new place, before we sink or catch on fire. Before we're discovered and scrubbed clean.

I tell Frieda to start rowing.

Breaking

"Wait," the girl said to her brother. "You're about to step on a crack."

"Grow up," he said, without looking at the ground. They were twins but already he was taller, enough that she was in his shadow.

"You'll break Mom's back," the girl said. She almost believed it.

They were outside People's Drug, in front of the mall. The girl sighed, then skipped away, from square to square. A large plastic bag, held in her small hand, crackled with each skip.

"Stay here," the boy said, lifting his head, straightening his back. "She's meeting us here, by these doors." He took caring for his sister seriously, though he didn't take her seriously.

"I know," the girl said. She wore a light blue dress that formed deep folds at the base.

The fabric seemed to float in the air as she walked. She suddenly stopped and pointed. "Look, isn't that Mom's friend, Mrs. Wicke?"

"I don't know," he said, staring at the curb on which he balanced his feet.

"Oh, look at you two!" Mrs. Wicke said, coming up to them, her hands placed together as if to pray. "It's so wonderful to

see you. You look wonderful. Why, I haven't seen you in ages."
She smelled of hair spray and perfume.

The girl smiled, though she didn't want to.

"Look at you!" Mrs. Wicke said. "You must be almost done with school?"

The boy refused to speak.

"We have two weeks left," the girl finally said.

"Oh, well, you can certainly hang in there for that long," Mrs. Wicke said and grinned a commiserating grin.

The boy didn't smile.

"I know that feeling," Mrs. Wicke said. "You just want to get out and have fun. Yes, I know. It must be hard. But I imagine you both are doing well. What brings you out here today? Are you doing summer shopping? I see you have a bag of things there."

"Yes," the girl said, "things."

Their mother pulled her car up to the curb then and turned off the engine. Mrs. Wicke walked around and hugged the mother while she still sat in the driver's seat. "So good to see you," she said.

"Good to see you," their mother said. The children climbed into the back seat.

Mrs. Wicke and their mother chatted a while; they were old friends. Eventually, Mrs. Wicke hugged her again, and said with a smile, "You have such wonderful children." Then she walked across the parking lot to her own car.

When she was a safe distance away, the boy said, "She's so . . . so . . ."

"So *what*?" the mother asked.

The girl cut in, "She's so *Yah and yah and yah!* and *It's so great!* and *So, you bought some things!*" She twirled her hand as she spoke.

The mother started up the car again. "Have some sympathy," she said. "My God, she lost her son."

"It's been over a year," the girl said.

"Less than that," the mother said back.

"No, a year," the girl said, as though they were debating something meaningless, like what they had had for breakfast. "It was a month before school let out. I remember, because it was just too late to dedicate the yearbook to him."

The boy leaned back, trying not to listen. He was looking at a dog in a parked car nearby. A window was down and the brown and white muzzle was sticking out, a pink tongue vibrating off the edge of the bottom teeth.

The mother put the car in gear, but held her foot on the brake a moment while she looked from side to side. "Well," she said, "it doesn't go away, not after a year, not even after ten years. If I had lost one of you . . . dear God . . . I don't think I could manage as well as she does."

Without turning, the boy said, "All the more reason to not be that way."

"What way?"

"You'd think she'd . . ." He closed his lips. The car was inching forward and the boy could no longer see the dog.

"You'd think she'd *what?*" the mother said, her voice beginning to shake. The boy adjusted his shoulders and kept looking out the window.

"What?" the mother asked again.

"I don't know," the boy said.

"What were you going to say?" she said and stopped the car again. They were at the end of an aisle of cars. She looked into the rearview mirror to see him, her son.

"You'd think she'd shut up," he said sharply.

The mother looked away and the car began to move forward, as if by its own will.

"I mean," the boy tried, "be quieter, once it had happened."

The mother drove out of the parking lot onto the main road, saying nothing. What was painful for her was that she knew her son was right. Mrs. Wicke's cheerfulness was not something to admire. What's more, he was only eleven, not even twelve, but he said this thing as if *he* had already lost a son. How did he know? He must have had some loss in his life. But she could think of none.

The mother turned right onto the next road. She was driving home instinctively. She thought of her husband, who had spent a lot of time with the boy. But the two of them didn't really talk. Her husband preferred to just *do* things. He would know nothing really about their son.

As she built up speed, she realized that she would never know what her son really experienced. It was tucked in the private world of his mind, strapped down by a silence that only children have. She could never see it, but all the same she had almost watched it grow inside him daily.

She glanced back into the mirror and saw the boy looking out the window. No one had said anything since his words. As she stared at him, he suddenly looked up and saw her, just for a moment. Then, consciously, he went back to staring out the window again, at the blur of road beneath him.

She would lose him to the world, she thought, if she hadn't lost him already, and it was sad to know he'd have no pity for her, just as he had none for Mrs. Wicke. Will I be just like her? the mother wondered. She pictured herself, older, smiling in front of the mirror before she went out shopping each day, acting cheerfully in front of others.

The girl watched the silent interaction between the mother and the boy. She had seen this before, many times. She leaned against her door, holding the plastic bag in one fist, thinking about how carefully, all her life, she had walked in the center of each sidewalk square, avoiding the crack. But for what?

Although the boy knew the mother's eyes were on him, he felt particularly alone, or distant. He had always had that feeling; it weighed on him. Today, though, things started to turn. He was becoming a young man who *knows* he is distant from the world, yet simultaneously that he owns it, or will own it. Slowly his quieter perceptions would grind down, like a speck of dirt nestling into ball bearings, until he would be nothing but another man, perhaps even a husband and a father.

The mother changed lanes so she could look back over her shoulder, to catch a better glimpse of the boy. But instead she saw only her daughter, the girl, leaning against the side door, folding her dress in tiny creases at the hem. *She* doesn't hold such loss, the mother thought. *She* at least will stay close to me. The mother drove steadily forward then, as though calmed by these thoughts. She tried to concentrate on the road, though at times she returned to worrying about her son—rather than what she was missing, hidden there in the folds of her daughter's dress.

The Origin of Doubt

I stayed with him one Christmas Eve at his grandparent's farmhouse. Brothers and sisters and cousins—all small children—were everywhere, running through the empty halls, playing hide and seek, waiting to open their presents the next day.

"Let's go to the attic," he said.

We climbed the loud dry steps, into the heat of the attic. The low-ceiled room was lit by dusk, a light pulsing in from the small gabled windows. We invented some game, to unwrap each other down to our underwear, two boys alone.

Our fingers explored each other, burrowing slowly beneath cloth. Below, we heard the children cackling and running, their sounds coming up through the floorboards.

"There's not much to play with down there," he said and laughed a little.

Them

They called her the girl with the big ears, though they didn't call her that to her face. That is, not to her ears. Not exactly. Not intentionally. They were sitting in the cafeteria talking about Mark Russell, the Spanish kid, the one you couldn't tell was Spanish, not from his looks or his name. They spoke over the roar of two hundred nervous voices and stainless-steel silverware scraping against plastic trays. The air was full of inflated seriousness, laughter, and insinuations that someone had too much—or not enough—familiarity with sex. This was junior high.

"He's only half Spanish," one of them said. Mark's mother was from Peru, his father from Omaha. Someone had heard him on his cell phone, whispering to his mother the fast marbled phrases of a foreign language that wasn't French. "It must have been Spanish," the one who heard it said. "Or Portuguese," another one offered. "It could have been Portuguese."

"Which one *is* Mark?" the youngest of them asked, swallowing a knot of fear, as she did with all of her questions (since at some moment, wouldn't she ask the wrong question, the one that would reveal how *thirteen* she was, not fourteen?)

"He's the one with his back turned toward us," a couple of them said.

"Which?" the youngest said. "They've *all* got their backs toward us."

"*Ahhh!*" one of them said. The youngest had annoyed them, just like that.

Nonetheless, they tried to explain, whispering, "He's next to the girl with the big ears."

It was at that moment, however, that the sounds in the cafeteria dropped to near silence, the way an audience hushes when the conductor raises his baton. Everyone heard the sentence, then the cacophony of voices returned, Stravinski-like, and within it, doubt blossomed:

The girl with the big ears had heard their comment and choked on her milk. She hadn't thought of herself exactly as having *big* ears, yet she knew the remark was directed at her. She made a note, deep within an unconfessionable chamber of her mind, to go to the bathroom after lunch and examine her ears. If it proved true (and how could it not?) she'd have to wear her hair differently, give up the hope of earrings, and not be surprised if she never got a date. It would be no wonder, then, if Mark Russell, who was sitting beside her, was only sitting there out of politeness.

She could not imagine that the reason he sat there, among the pale white girls, was to help erase within him that feeling that he didn't belong. He, too, had heard them say, "He's next to the girl with the big ears," and knew they were talking about him, about the ways they knew he did not belong.

And the youngest of the group, the one who had asked the question, said, "Yes, I see now"—though really she was still confused, for there was a boy sitting on either side of the big-eared girl. Both boys seemed simultaneously plain and foreign, and she feared she would never learn to tell the difference and end up dating someone who only her friends could see was wrong. Then she thought of the girl with the big ears, wondering if the girl had heard their comment in that awkward lull, if it might have hurt her feelings—though she did not worry too much about it, for what mattered was that she, the youngest of them, was back among the group, a part of *them* again. At least for now.

Lindsey and I

Lindsey and I are in her bedroom with the door closed, talking about pubic hair. We're wondering, does everyone's match the color on their head? Is it harder to dye than your head hair? Does it get softer if you use conditioner?

This, Lindsey tells me, is what girl-talk is all about.

I tell Lindsey that when I was young—I'm eleven now—I used to think it was called public hair. I could never understand why it was called that. She says I'm probably dyslexic. I don't ask her what that is, but I can tell from her voice it's a diagnosis, not an insult. Maybe it means naïve.

I glance out the window that overlooks her driveway, afraid her parents might come home and hear us, but Lindsey doesn't seem to care. She's sitting on her bedspread, which is sea-green and heavy, like the comforter on my parents' bed at home. It makes her room feel very adult. I still love it when Mom makes my bed with cartoon sheets.

Lindsey says she once saw her brother's pubic hair, when he was sleeping on the couch and his pants had twisted down and his shirt had lifted up. She says it was like scribble pouring down the center of his belly; it pooled up above where his legs meet.

I can almost picture it, and I blink my eyes, trying to erase the image. I tell her I don't think my brother, who is younger than me, has any hair like that yet. But I've never looked.

Lindsey's fifteen months older than me, two grades ahead, but we ride the same bus together and live just three houses apart, so we've gotten to know each other, become friends, waiting on the side of the road every day for the bus.

Lindsey pats the bed twice, inviting me to sit next to her. "Angie," she says, "I've got a secret."

I sit down beside her and wait. She gathers up silence, for suspense, then tells me how she once found a piece of pubic hair caught between her teeth.

"That's gross," I say and lean away, as if it were still there now.

"You want to know the gross part?" she asks, and then whispers it to me before I can answer her. "It was someone else's hair."

"How do you know?" I ask.

"Different color."

I wonder sometimes how we ever became close.

Lindsey says she started growing pubic hair the day she turned eleven—like it was a decision, a choice. "And you know what?" she says. "I found hairs under my arms before I even got them down there." She points to the zipper of her jeans and pauses, waiting for my history.

I'm tired of all this talk now, but I feel I have to tell her something. "I started to get them about a few months ago," I say, "though there's still not much there. I don't have any under my arms." I feel like I've said too much, but Lindsey just stares at me wanting more.

"I feel lucky," I say finally, turning my head away. "Because I still don't have to shave my pits."

"I don't shave mine," Lindsey says. She tugs the lower part of her sleeve down toward her breast and shows me her armpit. "See?"

I don't see anything at first, then I make out hairs that look like corn silk, lying against her skin all in one direction, like some current has washed over them and pressed them down.

Lindsey keeps her arm raised, her sleeve pulled down, so I can stare as long as I want.

"Huh," I say after a moment, like I'm no longer interested. I want to change the subject.

"I've got more on my other arm," Lindsey says, but she doesn't raise it to show me.

I stare at a wrinkle in the fabric of her bedspread, not wanting to look up. After we're silent a moment, Lindsey whispers, "Don't worry, you'll get some more soon." She says this even though I've told her I'm glad I don't have any. "And you'll get these, too," she says, tapping her chest, offering another diagnosis.

She puts her hand on my shoulder, like she's trying to comfort me, but it's no comfort and my face is feeling hot.

Then Lindsey lifts her shirt and says, "Do you want to feel mine?"

I look over at her chest. Her breasts are small mounds, topped with pale pink nipples, a color I've never seen before. I know for sure now we are doing something wrong, and I can hardly breathe. Still, I manage to say, "Why should I want to feel them?"

"Just because," she says, holding up her shirt, like an offering, and a dare, and a threat.

Her door is closed. No one's home. I look out her window down the road, both ways.

There are no cars in sight. I'm no longer sure what want is mine and what want is hers, but I figure I can't be blamed for doing this. I know I'll be called a coward if I don't. And if anyone ever finds out, I can say it was all her idea, since it was. So I cup my hands and place them over her breasts.

There's a shock of warmth at first, then uneasiness. What am I supposed to do exactly? I concentrate on holding my hands as still as possible, but all I feel are my palms beginning to sweat. I wonder what this feels like for her.

When I pull my hands away, I realize I prefer looking at her breasts, imagining I'm touching them—or is it that I imagine having them myself?

Lindsey pulls down her shirt and sits up straight on the bed. "I think you're a lesbian," she says. Her final diagnosis.

"Oh yeah?" I say. It's a word I've never used before, though I'm pretty sure I know what it means.

"It's okay," she says, patting my leg. "We're still friends."

"I don't think I am one," I say, trying to sound like I don't care one way or the other. We sit there on her green bedspread in silence again for what feels like a time longer than all the years I've lived.

"Here," Lindsey finally says, brushing my hair away from my mouth—as if she knows a sure-fire test. She reaches up and takes hold of my chin, then brings my lips to hers.

At first I'm lost in the suddenness of what's happened. Her mouth feels too warm and too cool at the same time— and more slippery than I could imagine. I think of the raw eel a woman ate in a movie I once saw on the TV late one night.

Then I think of that pubic hair Lindsey said she found between her teeth and wonder if it was a boy's or a girl's. This makes me want to pull away, but Lindsey is insisting and won't let go of my chin. For a second, I get angry—or scared. I turn my head quickly to free myself of her hold.

We both stay seated, but lean away from each other.

"The things I try to do for you," she says, then shakes her head as if to add, *You're so ungrateful.*

I don't know if it's the force of the kiss or her reaction to me pulling away, but everything has changed. I see now that *she's* the one who has been leading this thing all along. She's the one feeling something like fear. I think of what I could say to let her know I know this, to make her feel ashamed.

Instead, I say, "I'm sorry."

Lindsey smiles and leans back toward me. "It's okay," she says. "You're young."

This would be a diagnosis too, if it weren't so obvious, if it weren't said to hurt me just a little. There're lots of things I could say back to her, but I don't say any of them—because in my own way, I do love her.

Crepuscular

They were lying in the field at dusk, the tree line on the horizon looking like a row of teeth folded back behind them. A white scar of vapor cut into the turquoise fabric of the sky.

They had run away, from their home, their town, their numbing lives in school. Now they were resting, smelling the sweet grass crushed beneath their bodies, hearing the crickets and tree frogs emerging from the dark. They could hear their own breaths, too, and their hearts beating beneath their clothes and skin.

Everything inside was calming down now, but they were still sweating off heat from their long run, off the school grounds, down through the alleys, out past the last houses of town. They rested their heads on their backpacks, heavy with water and food and clothes. They held each other's hand and gazed up at the sky, as though they were about to be launched free of the earth and travel to a distant land.

The night darkened around them. All they could see now was the faint dark blue light of the horizon. The ground was as wet as a tongue. They felt the cold crawling into their body like a marshal of ants. Still, they believed in their calling, drunk on the giddy fear of one's first journey. They were already not who they'd been, but who they were becoming.

Soon, they would change everything about themselves: their hair, their names, their sex, their past.

But for now, they lay calmly in the cold mouth of the world, feeling the warmth of each other's body and taking in the first stars of evening as if they were droplets of nectar that would feed them through all the nights to come.

Taro

It's strange how childhood dreams and drunken moments blur together in memory like plants on the side of the highway as you speed past to somewhere new. I remember my brother Taro, those long days we spent together in the pool behind our house, playing Marco-Polo. He'd close his eyes and call out "Marco" and I would respond, "Polo," then dash away as he lurched forward to tag me. After he finally touched me, when I became *it*, I would lunge in the darkness, my eyes squeezed shut, searching for him. What a nightmare fantasy: blinded, restrained to a sluggish walk by the density of water, searching for that other body, held captive in the tiny aquatic universe with me.

Mom and Dad were strict about no playing in the house, but outside we could do what we liked. It seems we spent all of summer in that pool, calling out to each other: *Marco, Polo.* We rarely spoke besides those words, not even when we swam laps beside each other or when we wrestled in the water. Taro always beat me at wrestle. He was almost full grown then and could lift me above the water and throw me into the air. I would crash down into the water like a building collapsing, water pouring into my head from everywhere. Then I'd push up out of it, shaking my head and snorting out water, born all over again.

He was four years older than me, but nearly twice as large, and I wondered if I would one day be like him. Would we one day wrestle where I would win?

It's summer now, many years later. We're on the back porch of our parent's house, a different house, with no pool. Taro's sitting across from me, drinking a beer. I'm drinking one, too. We've been sitting here for an hour, drinking, him smoking his cigarettes with his grease-stained hands. Mom's in washing up the dinner dishes and Dad's off playing on his computer.

Every time Taro gets up to get a beer, he asks if I want one, and I always say yes, to keep up with him. But I'm drunk now, slurring words. I can tell because he is making fun of me. I drink this one fast, and stand before he can, offering to get him one this time. Then, in the kitchen, I fill up my old bottle with water, pull out a fresh one for him and go back outside.

I'm nineteen now, Taro twenty-three, and the space between us feels different. I'm catching up, though the distance will always be there.

As I hand him the bottle, I think, *It's just Taro and me here, alone, watching the sun go down.* But it's not sweet, like it once was. We're barely talking. The conversation surfaces once in a while, like a whale coming up for air, then disappears. The summer is buzzing like neon, and I feel him watching me, like he's caught me and now all games are over, forever.

It happened in the fall, back when I had just turned fourteen, the day our family moved out of the only house I had ever known, into this new one, here in the country. Dad was retiring from the Navy and wanted to be out of the suburbs. Mom said the schools out here would be safer for me and Taro, who would be a senior.

Almost everything was in boxes. All that was left in the living room was the sofa, a pile of boxes and the large Persian rug my dad had bought when traveling through Iran.

The moving men had been coming in and out all day. Taro and I were wrestling on the sofa, no longer caring about the no play in the house rule Mom had enforced for so many years. We could do anything.

After a few minutes, Taro pinned me down and asked if I surrendered. I said, "Okay," but when he released my arms, I jumped on his back, laughing. Taro grabbed me again, his hands tight on my wrists. He picked me up and carried me across the room, like I was something wild he had caught. He threw me in an empty moving box, and I collapsed inside. Before I could stand up, he folded close the flaps.

"Taro!" I yelled.

"Be quiet or I'll tape it shut," he said. I kept yelling his name, wanting to get out. He lifted one corner of the box and then another, tumbling me every way. I felt like I was in a drier, my hot body sweaty from wrestling, hitting against the dry cardboard.

Dots of light from the corners pierced the dark space, but I was being thrown around too quickly to see anything else.

Taro didn't stop. I tumbled and tumbled, starting to feel sick. I decided then to push in every direction, and suddenly, I bound out of the box, onto the rug.

The cool bright air of the living room. The itchy thistle of the carpet. Then, Taro jumped on top of me. I lay on belly down, exhausted, resigned, him over me like some immovable weight.

Taro started saying something to me, but I couldn't hear with the pounding of blood in my ears. I started counting down from ten, as though these were my last breaths of life. Or was it him counting, the wrestler's count down? I squirmed to make Taro believe I hadn't completely surrendered. But a part of me was happy, even to die like that, I felt myself pressing, not down into the earth, but up against the weight of his body, to feel it more. I realized that this was all I wanted— not to be him, but to be against to him, just as we were.

◆ ◆ ◆

Then there was that noise. I heard men, the distinct roughness of older men's voices. I felt everything move—we were being rolled up into the carpet! The wool of the fabric burned my neck and now Taro's bones—his elbow, his hip—were pressed almost violently into my back. I heard the old men's laughter. Taro didn't say anything; he just breathed into my neck. I couldn't see anything. It was darker than the box, we had no air at all. But everything was all right for that moment, with Taro there.

The men called our dad in and said, "We found them there like that." Then they laughed more. As soon as we were free and standing, Taro pushed me hard against the floor. I fell and stayed there, looking up at him, certain he knew what I wanted.

Soon after that day, Dad bought Taro the motorcycle he had always wanted. He made dirt trails in the fields behind our new house, riding the bike all day. By spring, his arms had grown thick from steadying the weight of his bike; his walk was stiff, hiding falls he'd taken. Then, at the start of summer, Taro got his license and after school each day he rode back into the city to visit old friends.

I hardly saw much of Taro after that. Now it's only once a year, on one of his short visits, like this one.

It's late now, the sun has long disappeared, and Mom and Dad have gone to bed. But Taro and I are still out here on the porch, bearing the cold in shorts and tee-shirts.

We're still drinking, and though I switched to water hours ago, I still seem to be getting drunker. Taro's staring out over the porch railing at the fields he used to ride over. He has a big bike now, a 750-something.

Like with the beers, I know I will never catch up. But I no longer care. My head is pulsing, as if I were riding a boat across water, trying to find some new wilderness to land and explore.

When the Moon Closes Its Eye

We were fifteen, the only boys in school with long hair. We went to rock concerts in the city, tagging along with your older brother and his friends. In evenings, after dinner, we'd hang out down by the stream in the woods, where the lights from the line of suburban homes seemed like a dull and deadened glow.

Here, the air was sharp. It burned our skin in late autumn, and we huddled in close to light our first cigarette, and later our first joint. The heat and smoke of the leaves on fire tasted raw and wild and free. I watched my breath, full of smoke, snake out of my lips and dissipate into the cold night air, like a trace of myself offered to the world.

I watched the wind wipe it away.

I watched you breathing out curled lines of smoke through the thin new hairs on your face. I imagined you an untamable dragon.

We leaned against a gigantic sycamore, watching the moon rise through the leafless trees, listening for raccoon and fox hunting in the night. We passed the burning ember back and forth, a torch to awaken us.

I felt your smoke stained fingers offering it to me and watched your lips draw in the fire. I wanted to be you; I wanted to kiss you. I wanted us to merge into one thing, like the water in the stream beside us.

I took your hand. We traced each other's fingers. My heart ran through the forest and the moon closed its eye briefly behind a cloud.

Then you let go.

We never returned to the woods. All the wild animals have scurried. And now here in this car, alone, overlooking our old neighborhood, my cigarette burns down to my fingers and smells like ash.

In the Palm of Your Hand

He pressed his thumb along the dry skin of the apple. It separated from the flesh in wrinkles. Before his grandmother died, her eyelids looked like that, papery folds over the bright blue worlds of her eyes. "You remind me of one of my old sweethearts," she'd said to him once during a visit.

The apple gave off a light breath, the smell of fields. As a boy, he'd spent late summers at his grandmother's farm when the flowers by the edge of her woods had dried on their stalks and perfumed the air. Brown sugar and hay, caramelized grasses.

Through the woods, at the end of the overgrown logging road, horses ran free in the pasture, fenced with wooden rails. His mother used to ride, before she married. She'd taught him one summer how to feed horses, by laying his thumb beside his palm. He practiced a hundred times, his young fingers stretched taut, the apple balancing on top, like a ball or planet floating in air.

The rough fence rails would press into his chest as he'd reached out to the horses standing in the field. Then suddenly, their mouths were at his hand, snuffling. Their heat and their whiskers, that skin, like along the inside of a leg—soft, pulsing with heat. The quiver. Their lips opening into teeth yellowed by corn. The juice of the apple and the drool of the horse.

Once, when he was ten, he'd come to the field with sliced apples and found two horses alone, lost in themselves. Their hoofs drummed across the pasture, forming their own storm— iron shoes severing the grasses. Sweet dust floated up. The one behind was frantic; the one ahead frantic, too. The back horse rose onto the back of the front one. The boy stared as the two circled, coupled together like one beast. Wind wrinkled the grass and the apple was tight in his fist. He never imagined the world offering this, a horse riding a horse.

Billy Tipton Day

I know it seems strange that I'm calling—I'm thinking *that's* really what you mean—what you meant—when you just asked me how I got your number, because even though you moved across town, the number is, after all, in the phonebook, so it wasn't hard to get—except, that it was, since I never knew that your parents' first names were Zed and Betty—I know now, of course—and wish I had then, 'cause I would have started at the other end of the listings instead of going through every last Johnson—did you know, by the way, that a lot of Johnsons are black? I didn't know that; I thought that they were mostly white—anyhow, there are a lot of Johnsons, even in a town this size—I started calling from the beginning of the list at 8:00 p.m., so I would get through them all before ten, when, I think, it would become rude to call—rude even for me, who you may believe has no sense of decency at all, but I'll assure you you're wrong—but now see here I've gone and answered your question, how I got your number, when really I'm quite sure, as I was trying to say before, that that was not the question on your mind, then or now. The real question is—and stop me if I am wrong—the question is, what the hell am I calling you for, since even though we did grow up together as girls and played with each other all the time in that field across from your house that's no longer there, even though we were best of friends through elementary school, and we slept at each other's houses—which may be something, I understand, you don't want to think about now—it's also true we drifted apart and haven't talked for a few years, certainly not since I went away and then came back, you know, as a boy, and even though I see myself as a boy and you, you are most definitely a girl, a pretty girl at that, I understand—really I do, more than you can imagine—that *you* don't remember me as a boy, or see me as a boy, and probably, under normal circumstances, wouldn't want me asking you out, or want to be my friend, or even be seen talking to me, or even talk to me whether you are seen or not, yet there is something I have to tell you, or rather ask you—and here's where I get to my point, say what I need to say, and let you respond, so I won't bother you much longer, that is if I can, see, get it out, because— well, do you know about what today is? I mean about the astrological anomaly, or the glitch in calendar time, how there's an extra minute today and how that happens only once every millennium? Yeah, I thought you might—I mean it was in the paper, and I know that seems not to have anything to do with me or with you; we certainly never mentioned this before, and of course, never lived through one of these days before, but see, it all ties in with—well, do you know who Billy Tipton is? The pianist? No, you don't know him? Well, he was this piano player some time back, and he had a wife and kids, though they were technically his wife's kids from a former marriage, but the point is is that they were a happy family, and his wife loved him and his kids loved him, and it was only after he died that—are you sure you don't know who he is, because he was a well-known piano player and made a couple of albums, though maybe it's more likely your mother knows of him, but don't go asking her now about him, because I'm coming to my point now, which is to say, that when he died (after he died really), they discovered that he was not really a he, but a she, though his wife and kids, who had been very happy to live with him, hadn't ever known—now, I don't want you to freak out or anything, but see, today, with the extra minute and all, just so happens to be Billy Tipton Day, and so maybe you can understand why I was calling, because—yeah, yeah, it's Billy Tipton Day—you know, like Sadie Hawkins Day—right, that Sadie Hawkins—so you've heard of that and you know what that's about, where every leap year girls get to ask boys out, right?—well, this is the same thing, only it's for boys who used to be girls—or maybe it's for girls who are now boys?— either way, it's their one day, see, in the millennium where *they* can ask any girl out they want, if they happen to be alive when it happens, which takes some luck, or some skill, or a bit of both, and I'm happy to say I've had a bit of both, because somehow I'm still alive, despite those guys in town who suspect I might not always have been a boy, or even the way you used to look at me in the street if I glanced over at you, which was enough to kill me, too—but I'm not dead, as me talking on and on to you right now surely must prove, and I have, miraculously, survived to be alive on Billy Tipton Day, to this very minute, and here it is, and here I am, see, calling you, because you are, of course, the girl I want to ask out, who I've liked ever since we were both little girls, and we picked flowers for each other in the field and slept over at each other's houses, and told one another what we thought were our deepest darkest secrets as we lay beside each other under the covers of your bed.

Without a Rope

My girlfriend Julia was the daughter of a cabinet maker from Minnesota. She grew up reading more books than her parents had ever read. Her mother, a stay-at-home mom, still shopped at the shopping center near their house. Julia liked rain and played in it as a child, never catching cold. She imagined she was invincible. Grace comes to families like that, who seem so unsuspecting, but it comes on bitter tar-caked roller skates.

Julia went on the road with her best friend Maggy when she was eighteen. They traveled across the United States like they were leaves in a stream. They ate at diners, stole donuts from the back of bakery delivery trucks, hitched rides with men older and fatter than their fathers.

(If you never did this yourself, don't read about it now. You will only feel longing. If you did this, of course, you will feel longing, too.)

It's like this. The tight rope walker sees only the tight rope. There is no ground below, no lion in the periphery, no audience. You cannot fall off of a line if the line is everywhere you look, if all you see is the line ahead of you.

They were this way, at first, Julia and Maggy, traveling a single spinning line, only it appeared behind them instead of in front. They saw where they had gone, and they sat, admiring the fist of flowers and landscapes they had touched and tasted. They reached California, sunk their feet in the Pacific and imagined them taking root. They could have stayed forever on the beach, but eventually, they decided to return home.

On I-70 outside of Limon, Colorado, where the state turns flat and begins the endless plane through Kansas, they rested by the side of the road, waiting for their thumbs to lure in a catch. The wind was strong, like it had traveled for hundreds of miles and had hundreds of miles to go.

Maggy's father sold business machines and put a hundred thousand miles on his car a year. Julia wondered if they would run into him, she almost hoped it, though Colorado was way out of his region. He stayed around the Great Lakes. She sang a song that had been on the radio that morning, in the car leaving Denver, near the trains they found but were too scared to leap on. She sang, "Oh Canada-ah!"

But she was thinking only of home, which seemed to hum now in every cell of her body.

They were taken in. You can imagine any one of a hundred stories. We've seen something just like it on TV, but never felt it ourselves. If you want to take a quiz, answer this here: is it worse to be Maggy, being severed with an old war machete until you bleed to death, or lucky Julia, *my lover*, watching her friend be taken apart. Or to be the one who found the limbs, strewn like chicken bones, amongst the prickly pear, some peyote hunter or ex-Marine. Or would you want to be Maggy's folks, experiencing nothing directly, safe in their suburban Minneapolis house, their lives forever stained.

We all believe we are angels or Christs when we're small. If we read the right things, we become the heroes of our lives. It's nothing special, it's only us imitating books.

Julia can't explain it. *Once upon a time* . . . He chose her to live over Maggy. That's the kind of grace that won't surrender, that arrives on the tiniest, unwanted wheels. He grew suddenly weary butchering and took off in his van.

By accident, then, Julia became the hero, which is how heroes happen. Still, flash bulbs and cameras the size of shark throats, circled her with flames. There was still blood on her blouse, blood that wasn't hers, blood that he had dribbled on her after his spell in the desert. *Drops of her,* Julia thought, before she could stop herself.

And when Julia, what part of her was left, got home, she took up in a house and waited for her own hero. She only read books after others had read them first and told her they were safe. She wanted only to hear language that reeked of the familiar.

It was years before I could touch her.

This Was My Plan

I would come out to my fundamentalist family just before catching a plane to Bangkok. I'd saved up for three years so I could drink Mai Tais, snorkel, and sunbathe, while I let heated feelings cool back home.

In Bangkok, I went to a few nightclubs, but for a small-town boy, they were too noisy and crowded. The beaches down south were better, but I soon got bored. Then one night I overheard some travelers talking about a monastery up north that taught insight meditation. Their faces glowed.

I figured I could use some insight before returning home, so I took a night train north and the next morning I stood at the golden monastery gate. A tall, shiny-white stucco wall surrounded the compound and within were several temples with pointed, jagged roofs. I decided then for sure that this was where I needed to be.

A young monk named Lek appeared and introduced himself. He showed me around, explaining the practice. We meditated together, and after, he invited me to lunch.

Under a banyan tree, we sat in silence, eating rice and curries prepared by nuns. Then Lek took my hand and held it a long time, touching each finger. "So large," he said. "So beautiful."

I felt my throat knot. It was the first time a boy had held my hand. We looked at each other, and I knew. Then I looked down and noticed tiny X's cut into Lek's arms.

"What are those?" I asked.

"When I'm bad," he said, releasing my hand, "I make a mark."

"Is that Buddhist?" I asked.

"No, it's my way."

"Why?"

"To stop thoughts," he said. Then he stood up and looked away.

"You okay?" I asked.

"I should go," he said and led me out.

The next morning, I returned. At first I couldn't find Lek, then I caught him leaving the temple.

"I'm here," I said. "To meditate. To stay."

"Sorry," Lek said, looking down. "There's no room."

I wanted to tell him that I'd also come to be with him, to spend the afternoons touching each other's skin and finding some private place beyond the chedi where we could kiss. How could the Buddha be against such love?

But I could see the stubbornness in his eyes.

"I have to go," he said. "May you have good luck meditating." He turned and began to walk away. He wasn't even going to lead me to the gate.

It was then I saw a new X on his arm, just below the others, and knew I'd been the cause of it.

Alignment

They lived in the same neighborhood, biked the same streets, went to potlucks at the same collective houses. What they remember of summer nights is drinking beer on front porches as joints floated through the air like fireflies, kissing each person's lips. Talking of Rilke and Descartes until dawn. Walking home in the rain.

Then autumn came. They pulled out old gray sweaters from their closets. They biked with coats and scarves. Evenings became large bottles of wine and steaming kitchens. Fresh bread from the oven. Everyone sitting on the floor, mismatched plates in their laps, the house dog meandering through the crowd like a hostess, looking for scraps.

One night, near solstice, a few stayed up, improvising an epic poem in rhyme. One by one, they fell asleep, on the sofa, curled up on the rug, against each other's bodies. The candles burned out, the night grew dark.

Then the moon snuck in. It brushed across three faces, the way a moth might glide past your arm. Each woke to the light, and without a word, they began to kiss one another. They had never seen each other in this light before. They kissed and kissed, as the moon trailed across their faces. It was like drinking milk from a distant planet.

Then their portion of the room grew dark, they grew tired, and, with fingers interlocked, they fell asleep. Later, when the moonlight slid across the dog's face, it woke and sighed a moment, then curled back up and closed its eyes.

II.

A House Divided

Fortune

Allie tugged the letter free from the mail slot, but the crease remained. Half good news, half bad, Allie figured—which, considering it was a letter from Dad, would be better than usual.

Allie tore the envelope open and read Dad's large, wiry scrawl. He had just won a new Jeep Cherokee through some sweepstakes and had to pick it up on August 1, in Washington. Could he stop by and say hello on his drive back to Wisconsin? Enclosed was a copy of the winning letter.

Allie's dad, it seemed, was on a roll, and Allie decided to give him another chance.

When Allie's dad called from the sweepstakes hotel, they agreed to dinner the next night at six.

"We can have something simple," Allie said over the phone. "Maybe Chinese."

"Oh, you cook Chinese?" Dad asked.

"I meant take out," Allie said, recalling that the wok was propping up the hot water heater in the basement. "You've never seen my place, have you, Dad?"

"I guess not. You own it?"

"For the last seven years. It's not much, but it's mine."

"Huh. Well, you've got to see this Jeep, Allie. It's gold and has quadraphonic sound. A beauty."

Allie's Dad arrived at six-thirty. Allie first peered out through a window, wondering if maybe it was better not to let him in. But when Dad knocked again, long and hard, as though he were begging to see his only child, Allie decided to open the door. They hugged for a moment, though they had never hugged before.

"Come look at the jeep," Dad said before Allie could invite him in. "The top folds down and everything. They even gave me a hundred dollar gas card. How about that?"

"That's something," Allie said, as they walked to the curb. "It's shiny. Very gold." It struck Allie then that the Jeep was probably the most expensive thing Dad had ever owned.

They stared at the Jeep a while. Allie's car, a used gray Honda Civic, was parked right behind, but Allie didn't point it out.

"Want to see the house?" Allie finally asked.

"You mentioned Chinese," Dad said then.

"Right. Well, we could walk to the restaurant, get take out, and eat it here."

"Sounds great," Allie's dad said. "But let's drive. You've got to experience this thing: the wind, sitting up so high."

On the drive, Allie's dad didn't ask about Allie's life, and Allie sensed there was not much new in Dad's life—besides the Jeep. Allie knew Dad saw this car as a swell of good fortune, and like any true gambler, he was fixated on riding this wave, on staying with it. Allie remembered as a child being swept up into the highs of Dad's winning streaks. Allie wondered then how long the Jeep would stay in his hands.

At the restaurant, Allie's Dad said, "You order," and slipped into the men's room when it was time to pay. Allie knew all Dad had to offer was the ride, and himself.

As they left the restaurant, Dad started talking about the new car smell, how the Chinese food might overtake the scent. "Do you mind if we walk back?" he asked. "I'll get the Jeep later."

"Sure," said Allie.

"I'd just hate for sauce to leak onto the upholstery," Dad said, locking up the Jeep. "Whenever I'd look at that stain, I'd think of you."

Allie smiled, but felt punched. They headed back to the house, Allie walking in front.

It was always this way: when Dad's good luck ended, he took Allie down with him.

At the house, Allie climbed the stairs, but Dad stayed by the gate. "You know," he said, "maybe I can wait on the food and walk back for the car. I just don't know if I trust this neighborhood with that brand new Jeep."

"As you wish," Allie said, gripping tight the plastic bag of food. "Just knock when you're back."

They didn't hug, but Allie's Dad came up and took a fortune cookie from the bag. "For the road," he said, then walked off back to the restaurant.

Allie went inside to watch TV and eat noodles. On the way to the couch, Allie threw out the other cookie, already knowing the fortune: Dad was not coming back.

Buried

You dropped it in the ocean so as to hide it. But no, that wasn't quite the right word—for hiding implies *from* someone, and no one was looking for it or would think to find it here. And hiding suggests a temporariness. One hides something, only later to reveal it. When one hides something for good, one buries it.

Yet it seemed wrong, when you drew the small parcel from your coat pocket as you leaned over the rail of the whale-watching boat that afternoon, letting it slip out of your fingers into the water, to think of that as burying. You looked around, worried about being seen. But everyone else on deck was looking off in the distance for a tail or a spout of water.

You watched as the parcel float, and after the water slipped in and mixed with ash, you watched it unceremoniously sink. As the boat pressed on, you could imagine the small wooden box swaying downward until it rested on the ocean floor.

Yet all that water did not exactly bury the thing. Not made of earth, the ocean could not truly put it to rest.

As a child, you had been unsettled by the phrase "a man buried at sea"; you couldn't understand how anyone could dig a grave at the bottom of the ocean, how they could pull the casket down, then cover it up. Wouldn't the currents wash the dirt away and reveal the body? When you learned that it meant they simply let the body slip off the ship into the ocean, you were repulsed by the thought, the slothfulness and incompleteness of the act.

But you now have done the act yourself, buried but not buried, let the parcel fall into the immense anonymity of the sea. And since then, you have not spent a day without thinking about it. Sometimes you imagined the parcel jostled by the waves or the tail of a large fish. Other times you pictured it catching the hook of a fishing line or the net of a trawler. Or you see it scuttling across the ocean floor, incrementally, pushed by the currents so that it seemed almost a living thing again.

They told you before he was out of the womb that he wouldn't live long. The arrhythmic pulse, a tell-tale heart. You said no matter, you would care for him until he ceased being. Then you'd return it to a watery place, where it might feel comfort.

But now you find yourself going to the shore each day, as though the thing might wash up on the beach. You believe it's not comfortable, alone on the ocean floor. It's trying to come back to you, even though it's only ash in a box. You imagine that if you don't find it, it will be discovered by a fisherman or an early morning collector of shells. Then, years later, you will see it in someone's living room or alone out on the curb.

When you are not at the shore, you find yourself watching what flows from faucets, as if your box might come through the small metal opening. You come to believe that all water is part of the same body, one endless being, like a grove of birch trees connected by the roots. You believe it might return to you from any source. You look at the sky when it rains, wondering if it might fall from a cloud. You look for it in a glass of water at a restaurant, in a street puddle, in the kitchen sink.

Soon it feels certain that you will find it, that you alone will find it, for you have buried it from everyone but yourself.

One day you wake up, certain that your tiny wooden box is still lying on the ocean floor, still as a stone, wedded to the floor like a shipwreck. It hasn't gone anywhere at all. You see then how well the sea, with its thick salty water, preserves the things it collects. Your box will never disappear. It will always wait for you.

That morning, you return to the shore, feeling it pulling you. You place a hand in the salt water. Without taking off your clothes, you step in, feeling you are a mother all over again, the cold sacrifice of everything. You start walking, then swimming. By effort or current, you will return to it, there on the ocean floor, almost as if buried together.

Breaking Tradition

Diana waited on the sofa, squeezing her hands into fists then letting them go. She'd sent her boy, Davie, upstairs, so he wouldn't be there when his father got home.

It had been an accident, what Davie had done. He was trying to help by setting the table. He had stretched to place a fork down on the opposite side, and his body snagged the table cloth. One of the wine glasses teetered, then fell against a plate, shattering into a dozen pieces.

It was almost beautiful, this bright, shiny chaos. Except that it was one of Alan's grandmother's crystal glasses, which Alan always hand-washed and carefully returned to the cabinet after each use.

Diana had cleared and reset the table with their plain wine glasses. She laid out only two settings, deciding Davie should eat early and go to his room. Alan's rage was infrequent, but fierce. Last year, she'd been left with a bruise where he'd grabbed her arm, after she accidentally backed her car into his. Later, he cried an apology, and she silently unpacked her suitcase. She told herself then that Davie was the line she would not let him cross.

Alan had loved his grandmother, and these four glasses— now three—were the only things he had left of hers. How the love of one person could lead to the hurting of another made no sense to Diana, but she knew it was how things sometimes were.

She had already opened the wine, but had refrained from drinking, lest she be in a better mood than Alan and tell him too soon, too casually. She waited silently until she heard his car, its particular sound; the closing door, the tick of the engine cooling. Then Alan's steps. She rose, preparing herself for the night.

Alan opened the door with a face somber and still, as though he had already heard the news.

"Hi dear," she said. "Everything okay?"

He nodded, but did not speak. Then, after setting down his things, he asked, as if just being reminded of cordiality, "How was your day?"

"Fine," she said, "fine."

She led him to the dining room, poured the wine, and served dinner. They ate mostly in silence. He asked where Davie was. "Upstairs," she said, refusing to explain, even when he asked again.

They had almost finished the meal when she told him what had happened. He remained silent; she could not read him.

"Was he hurt?" Alan finally asked.

"No."

Then, after a long pause, he said, "Then don't worry."

"Really?" She could hear the shock in her own voice, the judgment it implied. Alan could turn on that alone.

But he simply nodded and said, "It's not important."

She could not believe it, his lack of anger. She waited for it to appear, subverted and intense, but he remained calm as he finished his food, that patina of solemnity still coating his face.

After she served dessert, a lemon pound cake with blueberries, she asked, "Are you all right?"

He nodded again, but didn't speak. He could not tell her what had happened earlier on the train home. A mother and her son, who was about Davie's age, had taken the seat behind him. Alan had barely noticed them except to wonder if they would make much noise, if the boy would push into the back of his seat.

But they were quiet, until the boy said to his mother, in a weak voice, almost a whisper, "I'm breaking."

"You're breaking what?" she asked, annoyed.

"I'm breaking," he said. Nothing else.

Ice Cream Truck

The ice cream truck plays its four measure xylophone jingle over and over, approaching like a psychotic clown. You imagine for a moment pulling the shades of your living room windows and the noise will be shut out.

But it is the first nice day of spring, and you cannot shut the windows or pull the shades, and already the jingling is upon you. The truck then stops its music, the loud engine that cools its freezers now buzzing in its place. It is an industrial water torture of sound that seems to loosen your ribs and vibrate deep below your belly.

But now even that is barely heard over the sound of a dozen neighborhood kids. Or is it just two or three, talking with the shrill sound of a dozen that only children who are strangers can evoke? It reminds you of the sounds kids make at pools when they play and splash. Their voices are like sharp coins, surprisingly adept at drawing your attention and slipping into the folds of your body.

They fight, ask questions, repeat lines from hip-hop lyrics, though most of them are white. "Back, back, back," one of them says as a threat, and the others chatter around him. You imagine seagulls fighting over bread crusts, pecking the smaller ones out into the periphery.

Then there is a hush. They each are served. One of the kids actually says thank you. And then the truck inches down the street, its jingle turned off, a few coins heavier, a few fudgsicles lighter. Can you now hear the small mouths sucking on their cold treats? Or is that the sound of their shoes pressing into the sticky tarmac, then pulling free as they make their way back to their homes?

And here now again is the sun, alone, pouring into the window, as it has been all along, but how quickly it no longer seems enough, how quickly you miss the sounds of the ice cream truck and the children on your block, miss them like you would a phantom arm, and you wonder how you will ever get through the day, in all that silence, as you putter around alone in the house.

Flies

Flies. Lots of them. All over the table, in my coffee, floating, landing on my arms and legs, buzzing around like a hundred toy planes.

I'm trying to enjoy my breakfast, but I feel like King Kong. So I roll up the newspaper and start swatting them, until a dead one lands on my plate.

Then I cover my plate and coffee, put away the butter, jam, and bread, and go back to swatting. Thwack, thwack, thwack.

I have to say, I get pretty damn good at knocking these things off the wall. The real pleasure is hearing the faint sound of them land on the floor like tiny bits of paper. Killing is not so bad in tiny amounts, it seems to me, and I imagine that I might be able to kill a person this way, one gram at a time. And then I wonder, *What if the flies are really one body, just broken up into tiny soldiers?* A horrible thought—and it's a good thing they don't reassemble anything human. I don't think I could take trying to slice down a fly man, not before my first cup of coffee at least, not before my toast.

I keep swatting 'til there're just a few clever ones left: they fly around the fan blades and only land on the ceiling. I turn the fan on, and they scatter. Then one by one I knock them off, until there's just one pesky fly left.

That's when Judy comes into the kitchen and asks me what I'm doing. "Swatting flies?" she asks, then laughs.

"Yes, swatting flies," I say, not amused. This is serious work—man's work, really, the taking of life. A pool of adrenaline has welled within me and I feel myself now a man of considerable skill.

"My grandmother used to catch them like this," Judy says, snatching her hand once into the air.

"Good for her," I say, "but that would take too long." I look at Judy's hand, still sealed shut. Then I look around the room and sense that the last fly is gone. I know then that it has miraculously found itself in the palm of her hand. And sure enough, she walks over to the window, opens it up, and lets the insect fly away.

"How did you do that?" I ask, feeling a bit incredulous, and a bit wounded.

"Your hand just has to be in the right place at the right time," she says.

"Huh," I say, and sit back down, uncovering my coffee and toast.

Judy gets out things to make her breakfast: tea and cereal. I wait as she makes her meal then takes it into the den, humming. She sounds like a fly buzzing in the other room.

Finally, I sit down and take a sip of my coffee. It's cold. I unfold the newspaper, which now is dotted with blood, and try to read, but I hear them outside, tapping on the window screen, as if they are dying to get in.

Jealousy

Don't save your jealousy for too long, for it will turn yellow and grow gaseous, like old piss. It will develop a sweet, odiferous scent that can leak through even a mason jar with canning lid ratcheted on tight.

If you keep it long enough, a dark cloudy liquid will begin to swirl, forming something unmistakably solid. You might catch it in the corner of your eye one evening, a tiny, cashew-shape drifting in a miasma of fluid. You glimpse it curling into itself, then rub your eyes until it seemingly disappears—like the answer cube in the magic eight ball, sinking back into the black.

A few days later, you notice a small distinct head, and—could it be?—a quivering tail. Something is protruding from the sides—fins, or scaly arms perhaps. The thing is vague but certain, like an image from an ultrasound.

Finally, when you look again, it is all but formed, a small creature too distinct to ignore, too alive now to kill. You wish you'd flushed the whole thing down the toilet months ago, turned the other way as its effluvium hit your face like vipers—but you didn't. You were too afraid. And now look what squirms in the jar, its tail lashing against the glass, its horned head tapping like a tiny heart against the metal lid. You watch in infatuation and ask yourself, *Is this really mine?*

When guests stop by, you cover it up now. Only when the one you love shows up are you tempted to unveil it and thrust it forward, saying, "I made this, for you."

But though you are consumed, you are not crazy. You know that your love would run from the house in disgust and fear. You know this specimen, so animate and fascinating, is not the most magnificent creation of your heart. So you show it to no one, tell no one.

This silence is, in fact, exactly what it feeds on.

One morning, you wake feeling transformed, and you wonder, Is that monster finally gone? You walk into the living room to find, indeed, the jar is no longer on the shelf. You feel relief, until you see a thin puddle of gelatinous slime on the carpet holding up triangular shards of glass from the shattered jar. The lid has altogether disappeared. The thing has simply broken free. It now has reign of your house.

You spend the entire day outdoors, trying to enter the fiction of someone else's life. You buy soft drinks you have never ordered, take a Ferris wheel ride, and drop shiny coins into a blind man's hat. You come home late, convincing yourself that everything now is fine. You fill each minute with familiar habits—fixing dinner, clearing off the table, washing the dishes. You prepare for bed. You lock the doors, put on your night clothes, and turn off all the lights, save for your bedside lamp. You find the most engrossing book and read until you can no longer keep your eyelids from touching.

After you have set the book down and clicked off the lamp, as you stretch your hand up beneath your pillow, you feel with the edge of your fingers the canning lid at the edge of the sheet. Jealousy is here with you, somewhere close. But you cannot wrestle yourself awake. Sleep takes you away like a freight train. By morning you'll wake up, having been eaten alive.

A House Divided

Vicky had a painfully literal sense of equality. I understood this even before I entered our apartment. Still, it was a shock, to find the stereo taken but the speakers left behind, the lampshade gone but the lamp remaining, and half the coffee table left on the old Persian rug, which itself had been cut in two by scissors. (I suspected scissors because one of the blades remained, beside the bolt that once held them together—the nut, of course, was missing.) Even the bookshelf was sawed in two, like a magician's assistant, the top three shelves having vanished.

I knew instantly what this meant: Vicky had left me and had taken half of everything.

In the bathroom, the bathmat was cut, as well as each shampoo bottle, brimming now with gelatinous liquids. The IKEA shelving unit we'd bought together seemed fine, until I noticed that all the screws were missing—it stood by habit and friction alone.

I washed my hands with the half bar of soap, dried them on the half towel, and looked in the mirror, which, being a part of the apartment, was still whole.

Why? I asked myself. *Was I really such a bad person?*

No, but I knew why: *I* was not fair enough. I complained about her more than she complained of me, about how she timed the minutes we rubbed each other's back, how she kept track of the number of dishes we each washed, how she insisted I pay twenty-three percent more of the grocery bill, since I weighed twenty-three percent more than her. I felt like I was living in an Eastern bloc country, suffering under the tyranny of egalitarianism.

In the kitchen, half the utensils and cooking pots were gone, but Vicky had broken each plate and bowl, leaving extra shards if the break was uneven, as though she were dividing up the last bits of pie or lasagna.

I stared at the china and sighed. To be honest, it hadn't been the prettiest set.

I'm not sure if exactly half the canned food was taken, but on this account, I trust Vicky implicitly. In fact, I saw how generous Vicky had been. For instance, the food in our fridge was neatly divided. Someone less benevolent might have left a swamp of sauces, juices, and beer. And when I went to lie down, I noted that the bed was not hacked in two, as an angry lover might have done. The box spring was missing, along with two legs, making the mattress slope forward and slump, but at least Vicky had left it intact.

I sank down into it, not feeling cheated, so much as lonely. I knew I couldn't live with any of these things. They would all remind me of Vicky, of how thoughtful she'd been, how just—and how half-hearted I'd been in return.

A Box of Things

"She's a difficult pleasure," I said of my ex-wife. I was standing at the front door of her new house talking to her new partner, Sammy, a woman. My ex-wife, Lily, was not there.

We both took in the complex and awkward implications of my statement before Sammy smiled, her illusive lesbian *I've experienced more than you'll ever know and I don't need to prove it to you* smile.

I smiled back with a polite, *You're probably right* smile.

Then her lips curled up into something genuinely happy—I guessed she was remembering a moment with Lily or connecting some dots into a picture that pleased her. I imagined her saying, "Sometimes the difficult is worth it."

And I imagined responding, "Yes. *Sometimes.*"

And in that brief conversation that we didn't have, Sammy and I resolved the differences and tension between us and came to understand that we were never in disagreement but were simply choosing to look at Lily from two different perspectives.

At least that's how I saw it.

"Well, thanks for dropping these by," Sammy finally said, which seemed to confirm that we had said much more than we had said, that everything was clear. I'd come over to drop off a box of toiletries Lily had left at our house that

I'd only now gathered up in a spring cleaning, six months since she left.

"No problem," I said. "Enjoy this spring day."

"You too. And I'm sorry Lily's not here. She just ran out to do some shopping."

"No problem," I said. "I just wanted to drop these off. That's all."

This was the end of the conversation, but still, I somehow didn't turn to walk back to my car right away. I stood amazed at how much we could say without saying anything and how much we could share without talking.

I looked at Sammy, her unrevealing face, and then past her to the hallway of their house, where the box now lay on the floor, like a Trojan horse I'd forgotten to load with men.

Of course I had thought I would see Lily, thought I would see the appreciation on her face when she saw that I had gathered her things and bothered to drive across town to give them to her. Now, I'd miss seeing her reaction when she finally saw the box of things, I'd miss sensing if she appreciated me at all, respected me, not as a partner but now as a human being, the relationship we had been reduced to—or rather returned to.

Seeing each other as human is not a bad consequence to all this, I thought, and I glanced at Sammy one last time, realizing that I could—should—see her as human as well, rather than the woman-who-stole-my-wife.

But now it seemed she was staring me down, daring me to stay there a millisecond longer. The natural thing—or at least the civilized thing—would have been to thank me again as a way of sending me off. But Sammy stood there silent. Maybe we hadn't come to an understanding at all. Maybe she would hide the box and only tell Lily about my comment. "He said you were a—what was it?—a difficult pleasure."

Lily would shake her head and they would both laugh at my phrase. Then Sammy would add, "Oh, and he dropped off this box of half empty shampoo bottles." And they'd laugh some more.

I turned from the stoop then, unable to look at Sammy any longer. She had won, told me all the things she had wanted to in her silence, namely that my delivery wasn't worthy of a second thanks, that *I* wasn't worthy of it.

As I took the three steps off the landing, I recalled that phrase, *esprit d'escalier*, a French term for that ability to think of what to say in a conversation only when you're already walking away, down the stairs. Why do the French always have words for such subtle and accurate states of mind?

Only I didn't actually think of what I should have said in the conversation we didn't have. I only churned over failed possibilities as I walked along the sidewalk to my car. I wanted to turn back, to see if Sammy was still there, guarding their door, making sure I left before Lily returned. But I couldn't look back, and didn't want to give her the satisfaction of seeing me do it, that Orpheusian gesture of doubt and weakness.

I stepped into my car, closed the door and started it up. I sat in my own silence, where I felt I could not be watched, where I was protected by the glass and metal of the passenger door. I was about to pull out when I saw Lily's car approaching from down the street. Here it was, coming right toward me, the chance to see her, to step out and explain what my visit meant before Sammy could tell the story her way.

I put my hand on the door latch, about to open it, when I reconsidered. You will look like a fool, a desperate fool, I told myself. Not only to Sammy but to Lily. If you drive out now, you will pass her, and she will see you, and she will see that you drove on, either aware of her or not. She will not know if you passed her without waving on purpose or not. She will see, then, no matter what Sammy says, that you offered this gift, no strings attached. She will appreciate that. She will admire you for it.

And so I put the car in gear and drove off, willing myself to keep my eyes on the road as I passed Lily's car. It was difficult to do, but once I had past her, I felt a kind of pleasure, greater than any conversation I could imagine might have been possible.

The State We're In

"The landlord calls this color gold," I say as I lead the stranger up to my apartment. It is a fourth-floor walk-up, the staircase dark except directly under the florescent lights, where the paint appears a pale yellow.

"It's more like piss," the stranger says, a step or two behind me.

"Yes," I say. I'm happy that he seems to think like I do. "I call it 'Evening Urine.'"

He laughs but walks silently, no squeaky shoe or heavy slap of foot against the floor. One can tell a lot about people by how they walk. He seems a quiet type.

"I'd call it 'Unfortunate Place Urine,'" he says.

It takes me a moment to catch the pun, but then I laugh, my voice echoing up the stairwell. "It's a kind of purgatory," I say, "the stairwell of this apartment. I've lost people here. They don't make it past the second floor."

The stranger doesn't say anything back.

I wonder if he is considering turning around. But he must know this neighborhood, how the buildings were once high-end, how recent landlords have let things decay. I've lived in my apartment for seven years and restored some of its charm. My walls are full of books and art.

"Just one more flight," I say.

"And urine," he says.

"Yes, 'you're in.'" I don't turn around. I can picture his smile, though I can't quite picture his face. I stared at it for an hour at the bar, but now the image is fuzzy. The bar was dark, and there was, well, a lot of drinking. You order a drink—then the drinks start ordering themselves. And then you are climbing the ugly stairs to your apartment with a man who you can't quite picture. There is always the surprise at the top of the stairs, when you turn and look at him again, take in his face under the familiar light. It's not so much that the face is better or worse than you recall, but more how particular it is, how much detail is imprinted into the skin and eyes.

I reach my floor and collect myself, recognizing that I've been thinking in the second person for the last thirty seconds. I get my key out, resist the urge to turn around. There is always an element of trust in these things—that he will not pull out a gun or a knife, that I do not have a trap waiting for him inside.

I should not talk with such authority; I've only brought a few men home. It's hardly a nightly occurrence. But I feel somehow experienced, able to narrate all of this with a critical stance.

I unlock my door then turn around to look at him. A little shorter than I remembered—though we were sitting, so how could I know?—a little flatter in the face than I recall. His glasses are askew a bit, which is charming, and I see stray hairs on his cheek that give him a youthful nonchalance that I like.

"Here it is," I say.

We step into the living room and stand there as though we are a couple considering to rent the place. I look at my furniture and art, trying to imagine how they look to this stranger, but without looking around, he takes his glasses off, presses his body against mine and kisses me.

He is swift and forceful, not the quiet romantic man I had imagined. I feel suddenly numbed and quite drunk again. As he takes off my clothes, and his own, I wonder if alcohol lets you do things that are in your nature or against it.

I stand naked in my living room as this stranger licks my chest. I feel none of the interest I felt back at the bar, when all this was still *possibility*. I enter some dark, distant place, and my lust becomes as deflated and rumpled as the clothes gathered around my feet.

As he kisses me, I lay a hand on his back, gesturing for him to stop. But he doesn't, until I bend over and gather up my pants. He seems pissed. I would say "I'm sorry," but the phrase seems too obvious, and I've come to learn that at times like this, language is not always friendly.

We dress in silence, and I lead him back out, checking to see I have my keys. I have to be sure he leaves the building, so I walk down with him, he now in front.

His feet stomp down the stairs. The stairwell feels like a kind of purgatory, and I wonder if he will do something. As we reach the second floor, I think of the people I've lost here and wonder if I should turn back.

I hear him grunting or crying—I can't be sure. I think of the unfortunate place he's in, that I'm in. I say to myself, "Just one more flight."

As we descend the last steps, I feel the full force of gravity, of how far down I've traveled this night. I look at the color of the walls and think, I could call this evening Urine. I unlock the door for the stranger, whose name I do not remember, this man whom I will not now look in the face.

"That was shitty," he spits as he leaves.

"I'm sorry you're pissed," I say as I lock the door.

And as I ascend the stairs again, I think how badly the evening might have gone and laugh, thinking how the landlord calls this color gold.

Contemporary

We were at a diner, sitting across from each other at a table by a window facing west. It was our third date, though she didn't like to call them that. I'd first noticed her in a night class on American History, impressed by how she was always up on the reading and amused by the way she provoked the teacher with her questions. She was the smartest girl in the class, and the most outspoken.

Now I stared at her while she drank her coffee, admiring the way the strands of her dyed black hair almost covered her delicate ears. We'd been discussing whether the government or activists had done more to change civil rights in the U.S., and though I was losing the argument terribly, I felt drawn to how feistily she made her points. I'd never been with a woman so strong-headed and it excited me. I stopped arguing and just sat there smiling.

"What?" she said. "What?"

"Nothing," I said, and sat there silent. I realized I was beginning to feel something akin to what I think others call love. And so I said it, the most poetic thing I could remember from my English class. "'I want to do to you what spring does to flowers.'"

She looked at me briefly, then sighed and shook her head. "To quote e.e. cummings," she said, "is so early modernist, darling."

It was not the reaction I had hoped for. I took a breath and sighed. Okay, I thought, perhaps the way to win her was by not being so damn sensitive. I'd be feisty back.

"Okay," I said. "But isn't the word 'darling' early modernist period, too?"

She looked out the window and didn't say anything at first. "That was pastiche," she said finally. "I was using the term post modernly, a sardonic nod to the 1920s."

I nodded, conceding her point. I looked out the window as well. The sun was a bright orange mess on the horizon. If I wanted her to love me back, I figured, I'd have to be *more* ironic. But staring at the setting sun together didn't help; it only intensified my feelings. I confess, I had picked the table for this very reason, but now it seemed all wrong.

So I turned back to the diner and looked at the heavy-set, fifty-something couple across from us who were eating fried food smothered in ketchup and complaining about the waitress. I stared at the ugly plastic squeezable ketchup bottle and thought, *This will help*—that is, make me feel less romantic. Though I felt a comfortable nostalgia creep in when I noticed the bottle's reproduction of an old-style label, with the cursive writing, gold outline, outdated font, and facsimile of the founder's signature. It appeared just like how the ketchup bottles looked when I was a kid.

Irony, irony, I told myself, but nothing was coming.

"Couldn't I have been postmodern, and all that, when I was quoting cummings?" I finally said. I refused to look into her eyes, which were still fixed on something past the window anyway.

"You could have been," she said, "but you weren't. There wasn't a single ironic note in your delivery."

I glanced over to see if she might be smiling at me, if her expression might suggest she was only joking. But there was nothing. She was still looking out the window. I wondered if she wanted to leave, or if she were, just maybe, enjoying what she was staring at. "What about you?" I said. "You're the one gazing at the sunset."

At that, she turned back to her coffee and took a sip, seemingly nonplused. "I wasn't 'gazing at the sunset.' I was looking at the dents in the cars in the parking lot, thinking about the South American landscape destroyed by the mining of iron ore used in making sheet metal."

It was a strong retort, but what hurt more was that she wasn't even thinking of me, of us, or this conversation. I stared at her hard, and in my best sarcastic voice said, "That sounds very environmental of you, very seventies."

"Oh," she said indifferently, "I wasn't feeling any particular *way* about the mining—I was just thinking about it, being aware of things, you know, globally. I'm resigned to the world's end—however it comes: greenhouse gases, over consumption, or, whatever. I'm quite content handing the planet back to the lizards and roaches and vultures."

"Really?" I said. "So someone could come in and shoot you right now and you wouldn't care?"

"I'm drinking my coffee," she said, as if that answered it.

"So?"

"So, I'm enjoying my coffee. So, no, I don't want to be shot right now. But the idea of it all ending, sometime in the future—that doesn't bother me."

"That's convenient," I said.

"Why's that?" She glanced at me for the first time, as though I'd finally said something interesting.

I looked to the horizon, where the sun had finished setting. There was only creeping darkness now, against which the tall steel parking lot lights had just switched on. "Well," I said, "whether the world dies or not, you will. You've simply projected your own death onto the world for comfort."

"'Projected my own death'?" She made a sound, something like a guffaw. "What kind of Freudian mumbo jumbo is that? Is there anything you can say that isn't passé?"

"The past is gone, the future futureless . . ." I said.

"Oh, god, now he's quoting Eliot!" Her face worked itself into a little smirk. What stung the deepest was that she'd said "he" instead of "you," as if she wasn't even talking to me anymore. "All that's left to say are things passé," I said. "In fact, passé is no longer passé. It's all we've got." At this point, I confess, I wasn't quite sure what I was saying.

"Not for me, honey."

"No, I suppose not," I said. "You prefer to have nothing at all." I was feeling less and less in love, and closer to feeling its opposite.

She shrugged off my comment and downed her cup. "There, now I have nothing, and I'm content." She smiled an artificial smile.

"So, now can I shoot you?" I asked. It was no longer a completely theoretical question—a part of me wanted to do her bodily harm.

"Ouch," she said and stared at me, as though I had just stabbed her. "You know, sometimes you say the meanest things."

"But it doesn't matter, right?"

"Of course it matters. I'm a person. I have feelings. There's no reason to be cruel."

I blinked, felt a pang inside. Where had the nihilist gone? "But you were mean to me, when all I did was quote cummings!"

"No," she said, shaking her head. "I wasn't being mean, I was being instructive. I was trying to bring you up to date. You were just about to kill me. *That* is *mean.*"

I couldn't tell if she was right, or if she even believed she was right. But I knew I couldn't keep up, so I conceded that I was in fact passé, some romantic schmuck who still wrote actual paper letters and didn't have an iPhone and rarely used Facebook. But maybe not so idealistic anymore.

Still, when the bill came, I instinctively reached for it, to pay it, until she laughed at me and shook her head. "Medieval," was what she muttered.

I sat there paralyzed, knowing there wasn't a single thing I could do that wouldn't reveal my nature. She would even interpret sitting paralyzed as emotionally excessive, melodramatic. So I reached for the check anyway, and pulled out my pen. I wrote across it, "I want to do to you what spring does to snow." Then I closed the bill folder, slid it over to her, and stood up to leave. I was feeling almost up to date.

Reconstruction

The couple was excited to remodel their old Victorian which they had bought for a song—until, tearing down the old kitchen wall, they discovered the remains of the body. No flesh was left—only bones wrapped in a dress, a wig, and pantyhose.

The police arrived and photographed everything. They said the clothes were from the 30s, when nylons were still new. Then beneath the wig, they found a fractured skull and considered the case a likely homicide.

The morning paper headlined "Unknown Woman Murdered . . . over 70 Years Ago!" But after the coroner's report, the afternoon edition corrected the error: "1930's Victim a Man in a Wig."

Cars drove by to get a glimpse. The couple drew the curtains and sat in the living room, wondering what now could restore their house to beauty.

Sentries

The two men sit in bed, each reading a book by the light of three candles on the bedside table. Now and then, one will stop to share a sentence he likes or ask a question— Is your grandmother doing all right? Do you want me to reset the alarm when I get up? Were you really so skinny, even as a child?

It's amazing, Zachary thinks, how one can simultaneously read and think of completely unrelated things.

Eventually, Allen puts his book down, and Zachary does the same, as if sleepiness were a synchronized event one could not control, as instinctually timed as the migration of birds. And, without kissing, they lie down, heads no longer propped against the wall. Zachary, who is closer to the table, blows out the tall candle, but lets the other two, now only stubs, remain lit, burning the last of their wax.

The candles are set in ceramic holders that look like upside down mugs without handles. The flames hover over the tops like translucent heads. "They look like sentries," Zachary says, looking into the flames.

"Which centuries in particular?" Allen asks in a low quiet voice. "The fifteenth? The tenth?" He's not trying to be funny; he simply misunderstood.

"Centuries to come, I guess," Zachary says and laughs. What he actually meant is no longer important. That candle holders could look to Allen like centuries, that he could imagine such a thing, is what is important. He looks over at Allen then in admiration, but Allen has already closed his eyes.

Zachary suddenly wants to look back at the candle flames, to watch as they slowly die down—the desire is from the gut, unusually strong—he feels as though he'll be able to witness something spectacular, like a supernova collapsing. But he stays looking at Allen's face, certain Allen will open his eyes again, for a final recognition of each other before falling asleep. It is their ritual, their evening kiss, this brief meeting of the eyes.

Though Zachary has never put it to words, it means to him something like: I'm glad to have you next to me; I'm glad it's you I sleep next to throughout the night.

The flames begin to sputter in search of oxygen. They brighten, then fade, flaring and whisking shadows across Allen's face. Still, his eyes remain shut.

This seems inconceivable to Zachary and finally he says, "The light looks like a TV set across your face."

"Does it?" Allen says, his eyes—his whole face— motionless.

"It does," Zachary whispers, as he watches each eyelid for the moment it will lift and reveal his partner's eyes. But they do not lift. They are shut soundly for the night.

It's unsettling to Zachary, the absence of their nightly practice. But isn't life— relationships especially—about constant adjustment? And didn't he want to see the candles, sputtering in their wells of liquid wax? Yet now, when he can have this pleasure without guilt, it seems wrong to take. Still, he turns his head toward the bedside table— for what else is there to do?

And there they are, the two small flames. One disappears for a few brief seconds, seemingly extinguished, before rising up again, like an actor prolonging his death scene for attention. One flame does this, and then the other, but neither will go out completely.

Minutes of night pass slowly before Zachary hears the early wisps of Allen's snore. This man for whom a candle is a hundred years. He wonders if Allen was simply, exceptionally tired. But if so, from what? They woke that morning—a Sunday—after eight a.m. and spent the day working quietly around the house.

Zachary can't help wonder if there is some other reason Allen did not look at him, some hidden anger or desire his eyes might not have concealed. Or, worse, Zachary imagines, what if their ritual only ever existed in his own mind? Perhaps the man he has slept next to for four years was never the man he imagined he was at all.

Gray smoke plumes from the right candle holder up toward the ceiling, but still a pale orange flame burns, like a tiny transparent lozenge refusing to disintegrate. The smoke makes Zachary drowsy. Perhaps he will sleep now, with both candles still burning—he cannot imagine extinguishing flames that are so near their end. Maybe all this worry can simply be extinguished by sleep.

As he closes his eyes, he tells himself he is not afraid of the dark—or of what it means that Allen did not open his eyes one last time to look at him. Instead, he tries to take comfort in the fact that something is still awake in the room, watching them as he passes into sleep.

Holy Days

A few days before Christmas, Marcos was describing to Devon over breakfast a performance a friend of his was working on, how he felt obliged to go, though he didn't want to.

"What's it about?" Devon asked.

"I don't know," Marcos said. "Something about the holidays, something cliché."

Devon squinched her face, briefly, as though tasting something bitter. "I don't think the holidays are *necessarily* cliché," she said.

"Oh come on," Marcos said. "Of course they are."

They were sitting across from each other at a small table in Marcos' pale yellow kitchen.

"What are the holidays," Marcos asked, "other than cliché?" He drank the last of his coffee and set the mug down with a sound that resembled a slap.

Devon thought she might have seen a spark. She inhaled, knowing where this would lead, but she could hardly let him squelch her beliefs. "They're ritual," she said. "They're history. Sure, the insipid musak version of Christmas carols, the awful fruitcake—that's cliché. But the holidays themselves I think are still, you know, *holy.*"

"Whoa," Marcos said. "I thought I was dating someone

from the 21st century. Does anyone used *holy* seriously anymore? Except as in 'wholly in need of repair.'"

There it was: his attack on *her*, covered by a silly joke. Devon crossed her arms and leaned back in her chair, so that it tipped onto its two rear legs. She couldn't recall having done this since high school—certainly never in her own home—but here at Marcos' apartment, sitting in *his* chair under which was *his* hard wood floor, why not take some liberties?

Marcos, though, didn't notice. Instead, he slowly twisted his mug on the table, making a droning *hurrr, hurrr, hurrr.*

Wasn't that typical of men? Devon thought. When you were forced to do something to them out of spite, they really didn't notice, didn't have a clue.

"It's not like I'm Catholic or anything," Devon said. "But, don't you read any history in your seminars? This stuff has meaning that dates back thousands of years, across cultures. Solstice, The New Year, Christmas—whatever you call it."

"But we've changed," Marcos said. "We've evolved. 'God is Dead.' We don't believe what people used to."

"Well," Devon said, "maybe we should." She set her chair back on all fours and slid it backward a bit over the floor without lifting it up. Surely the noise—something— would get his goat. But nothing seemed to.

One side of the table was pressed against the only window in the kitchen. It looked onto a fire escape, unless you were sitting where Devon was now; then you could see a sliver of St. Paul Street—the bakery-diner across the way, the fire hydrant, the occasional pedestrian bundled in scarf and hat against the wind that shot up through the streets from the Inner Harbor.

"Do you really think about what you have chosen from the past?" she asked. "Or do you base it all on *The Foucault Reader*?"

"What are you talking about?" Marcos said. He got up and opened the fridge. He did this when he was weary of a conversation or had just lost interest. He got out the carton of milk, poured two deliberate sloshes into his mug and returned the carton to the fridge. Then he emptied the coffee pot into his cup and stood a moment—as though he was trying to find another excusable task to avoid sitting back down.

Devon waited in silence: it was the only way she could make him aware of what he was doing, besides actually telling him. When Marcos finally sat again, Devon continued. "What I mean is, you use this language, English, you use ideas like subjectivity and agency, and all that good stuff, all rising from the western tradition—even cynicism, for god's sake—but age-old rituals, like celebrating the end of one year, like just being thankful we exist rather than not, you don't want any part of."

"No," he said, "because that tradition has worn away. It doesn't mean anything. It's hollow, stupid."

They both sat silent then, looking out the window. Marcos' last word, Devon thought, had had a wriggling tail of spite at the end of it. She glanced over at him as he stared at the brick wall beyond the fire escape. He seemed occupied with something very calming, as though he were counting the number of bricks that had turned black over time.

Devon hated this, hated the meanness that occasionally burst between them, and how evenly Marcos could ride it—but she wanted him to see her side, she wanted to be right. "Remember last summer after the hurricane, when the water was turned off for a week?" she asked.

Marcos sighed. "I guess so," he said, but did not look at her.

"Well, you were so happy when the water returned. Remember? You even said how you never really realized what an amazing convenience it was."

She let this neutral memory sink in. "That's all the holidays are," she said. "Putting yourself in that place, imagining the water is turned off and then seeing how wonderful it is that it isn't." Devon had come to the end of her point sooner than expected and found herself suddenly extended out into time with no purpose. And the world—or at least Marcos' kitchen, which acted as its representative—rushed up upon her. She lifted her cup in defense and took a sip of the nothing that was left. She breathed out into the interior of the cup, recovering. Why had their morning turned sour, just like that?

Marcos cleared his throat, as if to get her attention. "So," he said, "being thankful is holiness? Just noticing is holy? It sounds more Buddhist than Christian."

"Yes," Devon said, exhausted. Was she conceding or was he? She raised her eyes just above the lid of the cup and looked out onto the street again, wondering if the day felt as cold as it looked. The walk home would take twenty minutes. Sometimes Marcos drove her, but she wouldn't ask him today. She would feel the cold, the particular harshness of the day, and then enjoy the warmth of her own apartment. She would make the day holy on her own.

"Well," Marcos said, "I'm not saying we can't be thankful for things, but we don't have to attribute them to *god*." The way Marcos said it, the word sounded dirty. "Most people mean the church when they say holy. They mean 'The Lord' at least. I think that's how it's commonly used."

Devon set her mug down. "Not always," she said, still looking outside. "Perhaps holy was the wrong word. Or, I mean, it was the right word for me, but for you—" She was becoming too frustrated to talk. "Well, I just meant other things. . ."

Devon pressed her fingers to the window pane. The glass was cold and yet it felt no different than the burning in her chest. Within a few hours, Devon knew her anger would wash away into some activity, perhaps a book, and this rift between them would sink below the surface of their lives, like others had. Things would return to balance. But still, she felt her morning ruined. She now only wanted to get out. Devon stood, lifting her heavy wool coat from the back of her chair.

When Marcos saw her, he stood as well, taking their dishes to the sink, as though he were beginning his day, already alone.

Devon pushed her arms through her coat sleeves, and began to button each button slowly while Marcos arranged dirty dishes noisily in the sink, refusing, it seemed, to turn around. He was going to let Devon leave in silence.

Fine.

She stared at the back of his neck, one of her favorite spots on his body, so long and uninterrupted. Certainly, she thought, better moments would come, but why did they fight at all? Then, as if someone else were saying it, the answer struck her: these arguments were exactly what she had been saying—her moment without water. They existed to remind her of what she and Marcos did share.

She took off her coat, feeling as if new evidence had been rushed into the court room, proving her irrefutably right. She beamed with confidence now and had a quick desire to explain to Marcos everything anew. But she stopped herself. Instead, she went over to him and laid her hands on his shoulders.

He turned around, a look of surprise on his face. His body leaned away from her, pressing itself against the edge of the sink. But she leaned in close until she could kiss him on the chest. Nothing, not even Marcos, could shake her good will. In a little while, after she had helped him finish the dishes, she would even ask him to take her home.

Genre

This table, the wine glasses, the leftover bread on your plate—
that's nonfiction; calling it "dinner" seems a bit of a fiction.
Your silence, my crying, these trembling hands, nonfiction;
that it's our last meal together, fiction. That you're attracted
to someone else—ok, we'll call that nonfiction. But the idea
that you can no longer love me—this has to be fiction.

Boris and Natasha

I had heard that before couples break up they often attempt to salvage their relationship by marriage or by having a child. Trinity and I felt we were too young for that, but when we began to realize, subconsciously perhaps, that our relationship was on the skids, we decided to take a cat, Misha, into our lives.

Misha was easy to care for and seemed to make the apartment more complete than Trinity and I had ever been able to make it. I begged Trinity to let me name the cat when we first got her, and told her that all while growing up, though my family had had dozens of pets, I'd never gotten to name one of them. She relented. The cat was her idea, so letting me pick the name seemed fair.

Already, it was looking like a good idea, and our relationship seemed at that moment redeemable, something almost luminescent, as it had when we first met.

I named the cat Misha after my Czech friend's girlfriend who I'd always had a secret crush on. I figured it was okay because Trinity didn't know her, and I figured it might make me take care of Misha more than I would have otherwise.

We were a successful young couple, in our own way, with our two low-but-respectable incomes, our homemade drapes, our secret songs for trash and laundry day, our film series tickets...and now our stay-at-home cat.

What we didn't know was that Misha was four weeks pregnant. She ended up giving birth to six runts three weeks after we got her. A week after that, she mysteriously died. I thought it a sign that I'd never see the real Misha again—a pipe dream anyway, I knew, but one that was now dissipating into the enormity of the space between me and the Czech Republic.

Trinity and I stayed up nights feeding the weaklings, heating organic milk and using Q-tips to clean their anuses. While the crisis might have brought some couples together, bonded in the face of tumult, for us it simply exhausted our patience with each other. It wore us out and made us give up. We put the last of our relationship into the survival of those cats, and even then, most of them died.

As soon as they were born, we had set about naming them, thinking this would increase their chances of living, and eventually, of finding a home—we weren't going to take care of six cats forever! We decided to give them all Russian sounding names, since that's what Misha's name sounded like to Trinity—I didn't have the heart to tell her it was Czech. There was Shostakovich (which we called Shasta), Andropov, Putin, Dostoyevsky (which we called Dusty), Natasha, and Boris. But despite the promising names, they died, one by one, still cold bodies weighing down a corner of the old blanket we used as their crib. We didn't know why and didn't have the money to take them to the vet to find out. We figured they were just too young to live without a mother. It was when all but Natasha and Boris had passed on, that I realized my relationship with Trinity was over. Only, I didn't have the guts to say it.

Still, I think we both knew it, and one day over breakfast Trinity said, "I've been thinking: we should each take one of the cats. It's only fair. And if you don't mind, I'd like to have Natasha."

I wanted to tell her I didn't want either cat—I wanted to say that Misha, our clever apartment decoration, our emblem of our success as a couple, would be my only cat love. These two Russian runts seemed only to represent the messiness of our long and sloppy descent toward being single again. But I couldn't tell Trinity that I didn't want Boris—I knew she would take my message metaphorically—a sign of how I never wanted her, or could never hold up my half of the relationship, how I had always wanted her to carry the responsibility of the relationship. I had a heart of stone, she'd say, that would never accept the soft furry kittenness of the world into my life.

I had to pick my battles in the upcoming war, and Boris was not worth enough to be one of them.

It's probably not surprising, I suppose, that three weeks after Trinity and I broke up, Boris died as well. Perhaps out of malnutrition or loneliness—it's hard to tell. I told my friends of his tormented life—a bastard child who had lost a mother and four siblings, and been separated from his last surviving sister. I got a lot of sympathy for his death, and of course for Trinity leaving me. I was feeling pretty good for feeling so bad. I felt even better when I heard from mutual friends about Trinity's story—nights up feeding Natasha with an eye dropper, the day Natasha disappeared, the day she had diarrhea on Trinity's favorite rug, the diagnosis of a twisted colon, the surgery, the vet bill, the expensive specialty food she has to buy from now on.

I felt lucky not to have dealt with all that, and I chalked it up to her making the choice of cats. Still, when I saw Trinity with Natasha, that day months later when I picked up my bike lock she'd somehow gotten mixed up in her things—I couldn't help but feel out of sorts, the way Trinity held Natasha against her breast, cradled against her body, the way Natasha purred against Trinity's shoulder. She stayed in her arms the whole time I was there, even as Trinity nodded goodbye and closed and locked the door.

A long bike ride shook the image from my mind, but that night when I went to bed, curled up on my side, I felt a longing I had not felt before—not for Trinity exactly, or for Boris or Natasha, but for everything, I suppose, that I had never fully surrendered to.

Abandoned

for Andrew

You are here again, in a large, empty farm house deep in the South. It is old and white, with green shutters and a rusting tin roof. The unpolished floors creak, the large windows rest crooked in their frames. You stand a moment, taking in the musty scent, and touch the damp dusty wood of the front door.

You have not been in this house before, but in others like it, too large and outdated to maintain, too stoic and majestic to tear down. Despite its size, it is a simple house, with high ceilings to draw away the heat. The long hallway through the center, with screen doors at either end, makes a breezeway in the summer. The rooms, you know, sit squarely on either side, four down, four up, with a kitchen at the back and a wide porch that skirts two sides, to keep it from looking too square and bulky.

You go from room to room, shaking free each door—for they are always left shut, as though to preserve the remains of the private lives they once held. Each time, before entering, you imagine what might be on the other side—a lavishly furnished room, a wild animal who's come in through a broken window, an old inhabitant living out its final days— or a corpse.

But you find none of these. The rooms are sparse, abandoned. You take in the browning wallpaper, open the drawers of the limp and crippled furniture that remains. You peer in the closets, and finally, you look out the windows at the fields and hills in the distance.

Perhaps you find a book of interest, a coin, a teacup, or an old toy. You hold it in your hands as you walk through the house, contemplating whether taking it is theft if the house has been forgotten, and will likely collapse in long slow heaves, alone and unnoticed in the fields.

Upstairs, you stand in the hall, imagining who once lived here, what daily life must have been like. Though the house is fascinating to you now, you imagine how slow life must have been, how boring. You wonder in which rooms people made love, what secret desires breathed in these walls.

And you recall a summer long ago, that boy you had walked with along the river, how you kept talking and walking until you were far from anything familiar. Tired, you both sat and drank the last of your water and ate the one orange you brought, and though you were hungry and could have consumed a dozen oranges, you shared it with your friend, and felt empty and clean. Then you two swam naked in the river, the cold water making your heart beat fast.

After, you both lay in the grasses, the hot sun drying your body, feeling like a fire on your skin. Everything shone and you had never felt so radiant, like the cold water and hot sun had awoken each cell. You lay there, staring at the blue sky, each pulse a quake inside you. You felt both content and ready to devour everything around you—the river, the meadow, the hills in the distance—the earth itself.

Then you looked over at the boy, your friend, lying beside you, the last drops of water shimmering on his skin, and you wanted to devour him as well—you felt it before you could stop yourself, before you remembered that he was another male. That long history of human passion you had been taught and memorized, but never exactly felt, suddenly made sense. You turned away, terrified at how strong it was, as though you'd just discovered that the sun itself lay within you.

You got up, put on clothes, told him you wanted to keep walking. Then you took off running across a field, your palms open wide against the stalks of grass, which felt like a thousand small whips against the skin. You did not run so much as fall forward, catching yourself over and over, wanting to outpace that feeling you had by the river, wanting to fall off the Earth and onto another one, the one that existed a moment earlier.

But you couldn't fall off the Earth, and your friend followed, like it was a game of chase, and so you kept running, though you were empty and tired, until you came to a farmhouse, abandoned and still, surrounded by fields.

You rushed onto the porch, drew the screen door back and pushed hard against the front door. You were surprised when it finally rattled open, the cobwebs anchored to the frame breaking apart like threads. You walked inside, your footsteps echoing in the empty hallway. You stood and breathed in the dust, felt the cool, shadowy air. For a moment you could almost believe this was the world you were falling towards. Or perhaps from now on, the world would keep unfolding anew like this, every moment an unexpected wonder.

Then you heard him on the porch and heard the screen wheeze open behind you. You took to the stairs and opened the first door you could find. The room was large and empty, except for a tall mirror covering the hole of the fireplace and the frame of a bed leaning against the wall. Your friend burst in behind you and grabbed you by the waist, toppling you to the floor.

As you wrestled, rolling across the floor, you thought of nothing except how maybe you could burn this feeling off by something akin to fighting. For a split second, you saw your face in the mirror, but you turned away. You needed privacy, even from yourself.

Whatever you were doing, whatever you would do, you could not look. You grabbed his leg, his arm, you try to pin him down, to free yourself from his grip. But you did not want him to let go.

Still, you arched your back off the floor and twisted around, and now your face was against his, your cheeks against each other, your eyes fierce and staring into his. He grabbed the back of your head and pressed your lips to his. And then you were kissing. And you thought, yes, the world is like this, one shock after another. But even then you didn't know what that meant. The shock of him pulling off your clothes, the shock of it being too rough and unstoppable, the shock of how fast you released, and how long he took. Then, that the kissing had ended, that he would not touch you any longer, that you were more apart than you ever remembered. The not calling, no longer taking walks together, the swirl of uncertainty and fear. The way your daily life now felt flat and hollow, the fear that elation would never come again, the months, then years, waiting for it, and fearing it at the same time.

And now, years have passed, and you have been with others, and you have been alone, which you are at the moment, in this other abandoned farmhouse, making love to no one on the floor of an empty upstairs room, the sound of your breath and heartbeat echoing off the walls.

That Long Evening on Our Balcony

Gabriella and I were throwing words off our balcony, watching them spin like maple seedlings or drop like pears, then split apart on the sidewalk. Sometimes a letter separated in midair turning 'mugs' into 'mug,' the s floating freely by itself until it caught on the front side of the word, changing it into 'smug' a split second before it landed on the ground and shattered into gibberish.

Two little girls were playing hopscotch nearby and we threw them 'daffodils' and 'candies.' To the man who spit on our hedge, we dropped 'ink.' The three letters soaked into his hat, and he looked up bewildered.

"I'm no kin of yours," he said, and we giggled, as we watched the liquid stain his hair. The poor man must have been dyslexic.

Gabriella and I drank gin and tea, a concoction her grandmother passed on to her, her secret recipe for surviving the long hours of afternoon bridge parties. Her grandmother would always bring a flask of gin mixed with a milk which would not curdle no matter what the proof, and claim it was her special creamer.

Here today, we use low-fat milk and only a drab of gin, but it takes to us. We pour ourselves another cup and salute Gabriella's grandmother, then drop 'cream' over our balcony rail and watch the white letters of the word spill over the grasses.

Next, I throw over the word 'rupture,' and we laugh as we watch it do just that against the concrete. The sun slips behind clouds, then buildings, then the immense curvature of the Earth, and all is orange and warm, as if only now to reveal that the sun is truly made of fire. I look at Gabriella and see her nose and cheeks glowing crimson and wonder if it is the sunlight or the tea that makes her shine.

She stands and laughs aloud. Then, without letting me see it, she tosses a word over the balcony she has had hidden in the pocket of her house dress.

"What was it? What was it?" I yell, bending over the rail to read the twirling thing. I should be able to make it out, for as it falls it grows larger and larger, longer and longer, but I can't. But then, before the word lands, it straightens out for a moment, and I manage to read it. "Century" it says, then splinters into a hundred pieces.

"We've lost a whole century," I cry and look up at Gabriella, only to see that she has grown quite old. The tea pot and cups are empty. The flask is dry. Then I feel it in my own bones, a wrinkled, crippling force, like gravity exponentialized.

Gabriella begins to shiver. The sun light is all but gone.

"Come on," I say to her, "it's time to go inside."

III.

The Fortunate

The Fortunate

There are those who believe that anything out of place is a sign, as if the physical world were a giant dream to be interpreted over and over. A woman playing cards discovers the missing ace of diamonds under the table and is certain now her fiancé is about to leave her. She throws the whole deck out in the trash, then lays watchful for a sign that she has skirted fate. On trash day, she has forgotten the whole thing, now obscured behind a hundred other myths and signals, until the neighbor's dog, whose name begins with the same letter as the fiancé's, is seen tearing open the trash, throwing the deck halfway down the sidewalk. She scares the dog away, but the damage is done. Fate lays out its hand, and it's a full deck.

It's not a particularly tidy block, so no one will take notice of the cards, except now, how can she avoid them, all those diamonds and hearts shining in front of someone else's yard? And how can she not count them, all thirteen spades, lying on the ground, as though they are poised to dig thirteen tiny graves?

A neighbor five doors down walks out the same morning and as he reaches for the morning paper, sees a jack of hearts beside his feet, staring up at him with the calm loyalty of a cartoon. How can he not think it's a sign, that he should be a lover, or that a lover is soon to appear? Unlike the fortune cookie at the bottom of the Chinese carry out bag that he cracked open last night, which told him he would achieve great things alone, this singular playing card seems as sure a sign as an x-ray diagnosis. It is delivered by the complicated parade of random events right to the steps of his front porch.

He begins evaluating if he is ready for this lover, or to become a lover. He looks up at the sky, at the line of moon so thin he first mistakes if for a jet trail. The moon is a jet trail, he thinks, and I am a jack of hearts! Anything is possible, he concludes, as the neighbor's dog is apprehended at the corner, gnawing on the last of several chicken bones. The owner yells over and over for the dog to spit them out, but the dog just keeps crunching down, as though it is practicing voodoo in the street, conjuring up the spirit of a chicken which will let the dog grow its own wings, strong enough to fly away from its owner, powerful enough to escape any force of love.

Fireflies

At nineteen, he loved Michael, who'd made them two flashlights that blinked in a specific pattern, like fireflies. "So we can always find each other in the dark," Michael had said. But they'd since broken up. Years had passed. They moved to different cities, in different states. He became a teacher, Michael a pilot.

Still, on nights when planes flew overhead, he turned the flashlight on and pointed it at the sky.

You Who I've Cornered

Look, I know some things can't be stolen, like the scent of a body, or the way someone nods, the green of the trees when it's June and or the food they dump into the trashcans at the cafeteria, but most things can be, even the fillings you have tucked away in the back of your teeth, like un-mined gold in some dark cave, or your ability to play a string instrument by crushing your hands with the metal lid of a trash can, or that smirk of pride that seems to be permanently glued to your face, with a quick, old fashioned punch to the ribs . . . so I hope you will reconsider what you said about me knowing nothing about possession and property, and start thinking about giving over the things you can give, before I consider taking the things you can't, because you're wrong: dignity is something that *can* be robbed from you, which I know because it has been done to me, and it takes not much more time than it does to take from you a pint of blood, which makes me want to tell you, look, that sunset illuminating the brick building behind you is something I can't steal, but the copper in those walls I *can* steal, with some effort, just like I can steal your head from your body—although the time it would take to cut it off completely, to separate the spine between two vertebrae and slice through the tendons and ligaments, that I could never get back. So, hand over the simple things, now, because I am, and you are, running out of time, and I'm offering you the rest of your life at such a low rate, it's practically a steal.

Current

It's 6:10 p.m. You may be dead, if the headaches you've been having the past week are from an aneurysm, as you suspect, and it has decided to break and smother your memories with your own warm, invisible blood.

I am here on a train, four days away from you, somewhere deep in Virginia, rocking beside stubbled, frost-bit fields and a slow, flat river. Bare black trees spread their intricate veins into the pink dusk, and far off, a single hay barn blots out a square on the horizon.

The minute hand of my watch drops slowly toward the six, hesitant to catch up with the hour. At this time of day, the Civil War suddenly seems possible all over again. It even feels as though a battle might begin at any moment, there on that far ridge, past the river, under the young pines. I don't know the river's name. But I watch it take the bank of trees and the sky and shatter them into ripples. It does this over and over again.

I bought this ticket months ago, before you felt anything wrong in your head, and last week we both agreed that I should still take this slow way out, though now I'm not so sure. Your pain may be nothing more than pain, a childish complaint from your body, just now thirty years old. They said it might be just an allergy or a pinched nerve. The tests you stayed up all last night worrying about won't be in until I reach you—if there is still a you to reach. But since I am writing this, here, now at 6:25 p.m., I have to imagine that you will be there.

In these long, steel compartments, where nothing happens, it's easy to imagine that everything is all right with the world outside. Trains seem like houses made for daydreaming. They let thoughts spread out, uninterrupted, like the kudzu spreading across that field. I look out my window and think of a hundred futures for me and you. The imagined future that catches me the most is one where we're living just outside of your town in California, me with a landscaping job and you still with that tiny explosive inside your skull. I picture us doing domestic things—taking the recycling out to the end of our lane, mopping the floor after the dogs have come in from a muddy spring day, driving to the new grocery store out on the highway.

There, I imagine we head toward two different aisles—you to get soup, and me to find flour. I'll be just a few feet away, obscured by tall, densely packed aisles, when I stop and think, *This could be the moment.* So I rush back to you, forgetting what I've set out for, and find you in the next aisle, holding two cans of soup, one in each hand, as if you're measuring their weight. I'll come up to you and say, as though it's the first invitation I've ever offered, "Come on. Let's get out of here." If you resist and point out the soup, still in your hand, I'll say, "Just buy both."

In the hundred other moments like that one which pass through my mind while here on the train, you are always there when I rush back to you. Until one day I come home and there's water, or wine, pooling around splintered glass beside your body clumped on the floor. I'm always shocked at the sight, even though it's my imagination that's inventing the scene.

It's almost seven o'clock now. The train is still following the river, like a shadow, and it wails its horn into the woods, as if to warn the trees not to come too close to the tracks. I see now a low electric wire hanging from the limbless posts, floating above the ground between the tracks and the green river. I wonder what sort of current pulses through it as it threads its way across the country.

Then I think about the blood coursing through the capillaries of your brain, and if I'll survive these four days on the train, not knowing what's to come.

We must have crossed the border into a new state by now—though which one, I'm not sure. All I know is that a new moon is appearing, its bright sliver presses against the mountain just ahead. The light quickly leaves the immense blanket of the sky. I keep telling myself, this is all I can know right now. I stare at the darkening sky, and have to be content with this. Then I watch as a deep-orange sun sets in between the joints of the furthest hills. For a moment, it spreads up and out like a spilled liquid towards the blue, then disappears.

Liana

Liana feeds me cinnamon cookies, a recipe she said came
from her Russian grandmother. We drink gunpowder tea
from a dark-green bowl with a thousand cracks in the surface
of the glaze and sit on the floor as the sun is setting, leaning
against pillows she's bought from Goodwill. The steam from
the bowl smells like smoke as it rises up through the
darkening evening, and the short blue candles perched on
top of clear bottles seem to give off more and more light.

We have just come inside from the dock out back where
the river lapped loudly against the wooden piers, and the
trees seemed to bend as soft as seaweed in the wind as it
came down from the mountains in deep breaths. We were
wrapped only in wool blankets, heavy and gray, and the cool
air slid down our bodies as she lifted her hand and pointed to
an uncertain place on the surface of the water where a ship
had once sunk. It had been full of sleeping sailors, waiting
for their leave at shore. On the far bank, she told me, there'd
been a missionary camp where the children used to climb
the wide oak tree and drop from its limbs into the water,
back when the river was clean and still.

Now in the room full of candles, the blankets still around
us, she looks away while touching the corner of the table

beside her like it is an ear or nipple, and says, "I can hold my own."

I nod, but I don't know what she means—or else I do, and I never doubted it, until now that she's said it, which seems to make it untrue.

"I used to think," she said, "that my heart was a clay pigeon, made to be broken."

"And now?" I ask, lifting the bowl to my mouth, the steam rising warm on the skin of my face.

"Now I feel it's a pie that was meant to be eaten," she says and laughs.

I want the tea to burn my tongue or mouth just a little. I want to feel some deep hurt. I see then how a strand of her hair has curled from being wrapped around her finger, and I think how it seems like her future, repeating itself, repeating its pattern, but projecting outward, forward, so that she imagines it is going someplace entirely new.

The blanket she is wearing is draped open and when she laughs as she takes a bite of cookie, the crumbs fly out like tiny projectiles from her mouth and land on the small ledge of her belly.

I stare at the crumbs and the hairs on her belly and wonder what in the world is not either loss or desire.

Voice Lessons

This morning as I lay in bed, my hand lifted up and touched that tiny pebble beneath the skin of my right breast. I discovered it Sunday a month ago in the shower, but who knows how long it's been there.

Don't feel it, I thought, resting my hand lightly on my belly, as though it were someone else's.

I felt my blood tap out its rhythm beneath my skin. I pressed my finger into the belly button, as if I could reach into the center and clear things out. As my stomach rose and fell, I thought of standing on the beach, how the tide rushes against my legs, then pulls away, how the sand erodes beneath my feet.

The furnace clicked. I considered calling the doctor. I've thought about it all month.

But instead, I closed my eyes and drifted, like the moment before death...

Stop, I said and forced myself up.

I pulled back the covers, watching as they revealed my body, with its tiny invisible flaw.

Don't say that.

I sat up and pulled a loose string from my blanket. After my mother died, I'd found a box in her closet marked "Pieces of string too short to use." As I slid into my bathrobe, I wondered how it would fit me if I lost this breast.

Stop, I said, but I went on, imagining never wearing the robe again, it resting on its skinny wire hanger until it ended up at Goodwill or in the alley.

Enough. After breakfast, I decided, I would call. I filled the kettle, which came from my mother's kitchen. How strange that some objects outlive us. I measured out the coffee, suddenly finding my free hand at my breast, my fingers pinching to find the thing.

When the kettle whistled like a siren, I stood, my feet cold on the kitchen tiles. My mother once told me, *It's a sign someone's dying, cold feet . . .*

Shh.

But I was already shaking. I'd had enough.

So, I did what I always do. *You don't have to call today,* I said. *You can call tomorrow.*

How to Bury Your Dog

You must start before your dog is dead. Be of firm mind.
Think about the graves your father dug for your family's
pets when you were a child. Think of the peace that will
come not having her sealed in a plastic bag and taken to some
unknown place. Think of how she'll enjoy being outdoors,
forever.

Next, consider: Will the ground be too cold or dry to
break? Are you strong enough? Do you have a shovel?

The hardest part is finding a place. Unless you own a large
lot, do not bury her in your yard. There are the neighbors to
consider. And what if you later want to plant? Finally, who
knows how long you will own your house?

Consider a large park, with trees and hills, if possible.
Where was she happiest? Where did she run the most free?
Consider a place with a view, within a dog's ear of a river.
But remember, you'll have to dig without being seen. You'll
have to carry her body there. Finally, look for soft ground,
away from large tree roots. If you feel up to it, lie down in
the spot and see how it feels.

When the time draws near, measure her, using a part of
your own body. Is she as long as your leg, from knee cap to
foot? Is she as wide as your forearm?

If you know she is dying, go there the day before, with a shovel wrapped in a tarp. In case you get stopped, have several explanations for the shovel: you are digging for rocks, you are digging for gold, you are looking for artifacts.

Measure out the hole. Then begin digging, dropping the soil onto the tarp. As you dig, do not think of your dog, the way her nails clicked as she would run to greet you, how she would bark, so happy to see you come home. Do not recall how joyful she used to be, once digging holes herself in the back yard. Instead, concentrate on pressing the shovel into the earth, finding the edge of a rock, breaking through tree root. Notice as you dig how the dirt changes from the color of coffee to the color of squash.

There might be large stones you have to unlock from the ground. The handle of the shovel might be rough in your hands, the skin of your palm burning as it rubs against the grain. You will likely start sweating. Take off your jacket if you need to. Take a moment to breathe. Take in the scent of the sassafras root you've severed, how it mingles with the damp scent of the earth and your sweat.

When you have made a hole deep enough, cover the grave with sticks and branches, then the tarp, and dirt and leaves, so it becomes invisible.

At home, find a burial shroud worthy of all her years of patience. Collect what she may like for the afterlife: a raw hide, a poem, a cookie.

The next day, after the vet has pushed the translucent pink fluid into her body, checked for a pulse, and left the room, pick her up in your arms. If she has died naturally, feel for the pulse yourself. She will feel like a different animal, her muscles no longer resisting.

Place her on a plastic sheet, to catch the liquids she will release, and wrap her.

Gather her up and carry her to the place. Do not think about what will happen if you are stopped along the way.

Lay her beside the grave. Unwrap the plastic sheet. Uncover the grave. Wrap her in the shroud and lay her in the grave. Adjust her body and place the offerings beside her paws. Then stand there silent, pulling out a hair of hers caught inside your mouth.

Say your prayers, then be still. Try to be as patient as she had been. As she is now.

When you are ready, take dirt in your hands. Feel how damp and heavy it is as you crumble it over her body. Notice how the earth settles on her fur, over her eyes. Use the shovel for the rest.

When the grave is full, pack down the dirt and cover it with leaves. Place a stone to mark the spot, if you wish. Stand over her a long while.

When you are ready, walk home, with the shovel and the tarp. Try to prepare for the moment when you open your door and walk into silence.

Another Story

I have forgotten my umbrella. A rain drop just hit in my ear, which makes me notice that a few drops have already sunk into the wool of my suit jacket. Now I can hear a drop landing on the dry leaves by my feet that have survived the winter.

Even if we walked home now, I'll likely get soaked. Joseph is up on that metal geodesic dome, playing with the other kids. We've only been here five minutes. He'll cause a fuss if I make him go back this soon. Ellie often tells me to let Joseph be Joseph. She says, *Don't make him wear a suit, just because you have to.* She meant that metaphorically, of course. He has only bright-colored clothes, cotton pullovers and pants. He only has two buttoned shirts.

I duck under a maple tree to wait out the rain.

A girl on the ground says it's raining and runs for the shelter of a concrete play house. She hunches with the round tubular doorway that looks more like a sewage pipe than a front door. She looks out at the boys, still playing on the equipment. One of the boys is swinging from a bar, but his fingers slip under the wet bar. He falls to the ground like a bag of clothes, and because he was not scared or tense, he is not hurt. He stands, brushes off his pants, laughs. Another of the boys has wrapped his body through several rungs of the dome's frame and is staring up at the sky, his mouth open, waiting to catch a drop of rain. I can tell Joseph is busy not looking over at me. He has a worried look on his face and crawls along the dome's frame with an exaggerated concentration. I swear I can almost sense his ears shutting down, preparing to not hear me call his name.

And now the rain is tapping down everywhere—on the ground, on the park bench, on the new leaves in the trees above us. A couple of kids giggle and one boy screams.

The other parents move under the trees that surround the playground, but do not bring their children in. Each adult has a tree to themselves, except the couples who have come together. We are still relatively dry, but I feel a few drops filtering down through the leaves of my maple tree, tapping me here and there.

They are all young parents; at forty-six, I'm likely the oldest. Perhaps they just want to appear hip and unbothered by rain. Perhaps they all think this is just a passing thing. There are patches of blue in the sky, and the forecast only called for scattered showers. That sounds so benign when you hear it, unless you are in a suit and have leather shoes. Unless you don't like any rain at all.

The kids are now on the ground, the rain making all the metal too slippery to climb. They are chasing each other through the play equipment, into the house, forcing the girl who took shelter to move into the house proper, and then out into the yard again. They are screaming as they run, one long chain of energy. Joseph is in the middle, scared and happy like the rest of them, that delight of horror we never quite enjoy when we grow up. It seems each child is the demon for the one in front of them, the last child happiest, chasing all the others with a menacing grin. Their cries are piercing, even above the heavy patter of the rain.

Ellie is an artist, an illustrator of children's books. I'm in one of them, a quiet father who says yes to everything, until his kids are building a boat in the living room and filling the whole apartment with water. Ellie says it's not me, not exactly. I showed one of the pages to my sister and she recognized me immediately. It could be a worse story. I could be saying no to everything, like I sometimes do.

Now the ground is getting muddy. One boy slips and his face is covered in mud. He starts to cry, but all the parents are laughing, and when he sees this, he understands he'll get more attention by being entertaining than in being needy. He wipes his muddy hands on his pants.

One or two parents call their children over, trying to dry them off, still deliberating about walking back in this weather. That patch of blue has left the sky. The clouds now look like heavy smoke.

Then one of the kids calls her dad to come into the rain, to join the other kids. He throws his hands up in protest and shakes his head no. But the other parents egg him on, and that encourages his daughter to plead more. The crowd is against him: he cannot get out of this now. He shakes his head again, but this time defeated, and heads to the center. But as he does, he pulls a friend with him, another young father, whose boy laughs when he sees him joining them.

Soon, almost all the parents are there, in the middle, dancing in the rain and mud. The rain is falling hard now, and everyone is drenched. But since they cannot get any wetter, the rain matters all the less. They seem not to think about the cold and sticky wetness. They seem to just imagine it as a hundred drums beating out a rhythm for them to dance. And so they dance and scream, the children and their parents.

Joseph is there too, on the edge of the group, but he seems to only be pretending to dance. He shuffles his feet a little, then stops, looks around, sees that almost everyone else is lost in the dance, and returns to dancing a moment. He knows I am watching. I imagine he both wants me to join him and is frightened by the prospect. He loves me fiercely, but I sense he already knows I'm not quite like his friends' dads. I don't play like they do. I stand in a suit, out of the rain.

And as I stand, I imagine being a character in one of Ellie's children's books, a father refusing to play in the rain with his child. Of course, in her story, the boy would be dancing wildly and begging, like that girl did a minute ago, for his father to join him.

At first, the father would refuse, but soon, all the kids would call for him to come. The other parents would join in and start to shout his name as well. They would shout and shout, until, of course, the father would eventually join in—because it's a children's story, so how could he not?

And I can imagine it all going like that; I can imagine being drawn in by all that attention. But here in the playground in the pouring rain, Joseph is not dancing wildly. He does not beg for me to join him. He does not even look my way. The other kids do not try to get me to join them, neither do their parents. They do not call my name. They are all shouting in the rain, but they are not shouting for me.

Christmas

Christmas Day is stress-free when you're traveling through West Africa. Family, and those you left who had hopes of romance, are only letters now, piling up in poste restante at the central office in Ougadougou. You can look out this guest house screen window, past the tapping mosquitoes and the box-like concrete houses, past the tents that hemorrhage out of this remote town—you can look right up to the purple edge of dawn, and feel nothing but peace. You are suspended, whole, standing up-right on the cigarette-burned linoleum, barefoot, with your hands on the sill, each knuckle looking like the barren hills you rode past for days to reach this place.

It should feel like peace, this independence. Except, along the edge of the wall, where a furry line of green mold forms a worm over the yellow paint, there are the words penciled by someone, like yourself, who once stood in this same unlit room. They say: *Jesus, get me out of here.*

Portraits of a Woman

A woman sits in a painter's studio, looking out the window at the street below. She has her own life—a job, a new red Fiat, a lover she sees on alternate weekends—but as she sits here for her painter friend, who she wishes were her lover, examining the ever-shifting scene of pedestrians and cars below, she feels herself a different woman, a character, perhaps in a novel. As that character, she feels the hollow calm of someone who has just made a life-altering decision—sharing a deep lonely secret, getting in touch with a lost daughter, finally breaking up with her spouse.

The woman sitting for the artist (how lovely, his long, thick hair) does not have a spouse or daughter, but she is certain the woman she is imagining herself to be has both. And she knows this character is from another century, as no one these days looks out a window for quite so long, considers their life quite so seriously, so existentially, as she is now.

A few feet away from her, the artist focuses on the portrait, knowing it is likely the last session. He chose his friend to sit for him because he considered her an elegant woman, someone with a distinct nose line. Yet, as he has progressed, he's struggled with what he knows about this woman, who is too morose or desperate for the portrait he wants to paint.

He knows she wants to sleep with him, though she is too old—nearly fifty! But at least she knows this. There will be no scene at the end of the session. She has offered herself up as a subject, and that will be the only way he takes her.

When he looks at her from the right angle, in the right way, he can see the woman he wants to paint—not his friend, though the two might look similar to the unobservant eye. If he can erase all knowledge of her, her history, her middle-class attachments (evidenced by the expensive scarves and that cherry-red car), then he can find within her face the image of the woman he wants to capture.

At times, the woman wonders why she agreed to sit for the artist, when nothing will come of it. She wonders how she will fill her afternoons once the artist no longer needs her. Yet, what can a woman her age offer but her time to someone like him? And, to be looked at for hours by one you admire, to look away from him knowing his gaze is upon you—to be so much the object of attention—well, isn't that half of romance? And some would say—she has said it herself—the better half.

She thinks of her bright-red Fiat, which usually gives her pleasure, a sense that she is still *new* in the world, alluring, and in charge, then imagines driving it home alone. So she returns to imagining herself the character in a novel. How easy it is for that life to feel more real than her own. She stares out the window, as her character, and surrenders herself to the world. She can feel that the peak of life is in some ways over, that there is only this private nostalgia to hold on to.

The artist stares mostly at the canvas, glancing only occasionally at the woman. He spends more time looking, and less and less time bringing the brush to the canvas. He adjusts slightly the brightness in a spot where the sheen of the window overpowers her face. To change too much risks destroying what the painting has become, how the hues are all talking to each other. He knows it is nearly done, which is to say, it soon will no longer let him touch it.

For a moment, he believes what is on the canvas is close to what he wanted, the vision in his head, though the more he stares, the more he sees it does not exactly capture the woman he envisioned. It is not his friend, nor his vision of his friend, but someone else altogether.

Sitting here day after day, for two hours straight with only one short break—believing that stoicism is another quality the artist will admire—makes the model feel empty. Why has she spent the time imagining being someone else, someone in a novel she has not read or written—that is, someone in a hypothetical novel that could only have been written in the past? By becoming a person who doesn't exist, never existed, and never will exist, has she simply been erasing herself? Is this a form of suicide, or just idle entertainment?

Or has imagining herself a character somehow made it real, perhaps even manifested itself on the canvas?

The woman in the painting appears distant. If there is a sadness in her eyes, there is a greater resolution not to let it overwhelm her. She is not mysterious so much as reluctant, reticent. She owns the room in which she sits and it's clear that the view she is looking down upon—not visible in the painting—is one she's known for years.

The painter sees now how the room in the painting is not his studio—it has taken on a different quality. It is *her* room now, and when he looks into it, he feels he is the outsider, an intruder.

He stares a while longer, then finally nods and announces that it's done.

The woman hears the words, but does not move her head or change her glance. She is completely someone else now and feels, suddenly gathered within her, all the time in the world. She goes on sitting still, looking out the window, deciding who she is and what she will do next.

Chicken

She was elderly, Chinese, and boarded the bus slowly, a live chicken head poking out of her shopping bag.

"No live animals," the driver said, but she didn't understand. She had only come to this country three years ago, to live with her son. She felt she was too old to learn a new language. She never left the apartment, except to shop, as she was today, in Chinatown. She spoke to the driver in Mandarin and showed him her transfer, hoping this would work.

"No live animals," he said, blocking her way.

A passenger nearby translated, pointing to her bag.

The woman stared at the translator then, not quiet believing his words. She shook with rage. What was wrong with these people? She would never like this country, never understand it. But her son, he was always telling her, *Just try, try and get along.*

So she lowered her bag in silence, snapped the chicken's neck, and took a seat at the back of the bus.

Keeping Us at Bay

We are gathered together—Said, Mohammed, Sarhang, and I—our arms around each other's shoulders, hunched in close. We have not come to strategize, but to pray. We are wearing our regulation orange jumpsuits which make us drip sweat in the battering heat of the Caribbean sun. We can smell each other's sweat, which smells to us cleaner than the sweat of the guards, who we sometimes are wrenched up close against—or under— when we're pressed to the ground.

Right now there are many of them around, having circled us at the edge of the lot surrounded in chain-link. They slouch, as we have come to understand Americans often do, even in the most demanding moments. Their hands rest on their pistols and tasers, or latch on to the chain link behind them, to steady their bodies. They resemble hyenas, staring at prey that is close but out of reach. They talk in small groups, opening and closing their jaws as if they are chewing gum. We can tell by the way they shift their legs and scratch at their hair that they are troubled by us.

We have, of course, spent years here, often being troubled by them. But now, we are not worried, about any of them. We pray, and the power, we know, is in our hands. There is less than a minute left. We are leading by six points, and the ball is ours. Praise Allah. It is a glorious day.

Half Your Age and Twice as Wise

After tenth grade, I prayed to God, if he would just give me a boyfriend, someone to take care of, then I would be faithful to him for the rest of my life.

I wouldn't cheat on him, like Elizabeth Ferrington did with her boyfriend, or tire of him like Martha Winslow did with hers. I would be as grateful as a person brought back from the grave, and if we ever broke up, it would be because of him, not me.

Before your first boyfriend, you live an eternity of life called *single*. You come into being, and all the days you know are lived alone. A date is like a rebirth; having someone say they like you is like nirvana. I was convinced of this at sixteen.

But now look. I'm not married, though there were a few opportunities over the years. I'm thirty-two—twice the age I was then—and I'm in deep, separately, with two different men. Two men, and I have to choose between them.

If I were sixteen and met the present me, I would squint my eyes in scorn and wonder how someone like me—who seemed no longer to have youth or integrity—could attract anyone at all.

But being thirty-two, if I saw an expression like that on a young girl's face, I'd pull her aside, my hand wrapping tight around her arms, and take her off to some private space. I'd say, "Look, what do you know about love? You're only sixteen. You can only imagine it. You talk about love like it's some wondrous, exotic country, but if you were standing in its streets, you wouldn't even be able to order a glass of water."

I would be angry, seeing the look on that girl's face, the girl I once was. I would tell her she has no idea how it is. I would tell her she has to learn—that it is how we sink into our bodies over time that draws men to us.

And if she said something in disgust about me dividing my love, I would hold her arm more tightly and say, "You know, love is peculiar and unchained—like a neglected yard dog. It can bite you more than once. It can bite you in different places."

And she would draw quiet, not quite understanding. She'd constrict her eyes further with conviction, then adopt a silence quieter than the nothing she has already said.

And so I would tell her about Marty, the way he laughs at his own jokes and how he puts the pits of olives on my plate, as though they are treasures, then grins with the meat in his mouth and says, "Olive juice, olive juice," like he's saying, "I love you." I'd tell her how in a hundred other ways, he pretends to seduce me. And because he knows he's not really trying, he's succeeding.

And I would tell her how when we have sex, we open each other up like blossoms.

She would be offended, and curious—enthralled really, for the little I would have said would already be beyond her imagination, though she believes she imagines more than could ever happen to her. Her eyes would widen a little, like they were adjusting to light, and she would wonder to herself—or say it—"Isn't that enough?"

She would say (for sure), all honest and absolute, "If I had all that, nothing would make me want another man." She would ask how it happened, that I got two lovers, and I would tell her, "I will not talk about history; only love. We don't have time for stories. There's a decision to be made."

She would lift one brow, as if to ask, *Are you telling the truth at all?* With the gesture she would be saying, too, that she wanted to hear more, that she would have to decide for herself.

And so I would say, yes, yes, I'm telling the truth. And I would tell her then of Seth, whose skin is as soft as cream cheese, who plants mysterious seeds in the soil around my house so I have secret flowers in the spring. Who sews back together the frayed edges of my favorite pants he finds in the trash. I would tell her how the heat of his mouth, then the touch of his whiskers, then the hot inscription of his tongue tracing the edge of my ribs sends me to new geographies.

She will furrow her brow, in anger, disbelief, and envy.

I will recognize each distinct pain in the gesture. And I will ask her, "Do you understand now what it means to choose?"

Stepping back, she will retract from me, indignant. "Choose either," she'll say, even if she doesn't manage to get it into words. "It doesn't matter; they're both more than you deserve."

"No," I will say back. "You and I, we deserve even more than this. Respect means believing you're worth it all."

But by now, it will be as though *I* am talking in a foreign language to her. She will give me a look, the movement of which I know so well. I could time it to a fraction of a second, the downward glance, then the looking away.

There's nothing I can do now. Yet, I'll say it—knowing she won't hear me, "And this is only what I know so far. I'm sure there's much more."

She'll shrug, shake her head. She'll be far away from me now, praying she never grows up to be anything like the woman I am.

In China

In China they recently completed a dam that flooded a hundred villages. Everyone was forced to relocate, their houses left behind. I read about it this morning while Mom was sleeping.

Each day I read the paper, looking for such disasters—piles of bodies in Rwanda, an earthquake in Chiapas, a derailed train outside Copenhagen. The worst news makes me feel a little better, lessens the feeling of dread.

Once, while I was reading about a building that had collapsed in New Delhi, I heard Mom start up her dry, sore morning cough. I waited to see if it would stop, without having to feed her a teaspoon of cola or lift her up to massage the tiny cords of muscle that still straddle her spine.

Because of a structural flaw, one of the I-beams that spanned the basement of the building crumpled around five o'clock in the morning, when all the tenants were still asleep. They were crushed beneath their ceilings and their neighbors' belongings. The few survivors laid beneath the rubble for seventy hours before being exhumed.

I had almost finished that article when I heard Mom's cough harshen, so I got up, held the metal pan out to catch the orangish fluid that oozed out of her lips, then fed her drops of morphine until she fell back asleep.

This was the first morning in weeks I'd gotten through most of the paper without her waking. The article I was reading said for five years the Chinese had been building the dam so far down stream that no one could hear the trucks of concrete moving in, like a string of ants, dumping their wet cargo against the wooden frame of the dam.

When the officials knocked on the town people's doors, everything was in place. The trees had been shaved like hairs from the hillsides, the timber already sold. There was nothing anyone could do.

I set the paper down to check on Mom. She was still asleep, her face for once without its grimace of pain, which seemed almost impossible to imagine. I placed a finger by her nostrils, to make sure there was still breath, then I returned to the kitchen to read more.

When the last of the residents were evacuated, officials let the water flood up valley, into each town. Most of the furniture and cupboards had been left behind. What wasn't anchored down, floated away. What was secure or heavy, simply disappeared beneath the surface.

This story, I supposed, was not as horrible as others. No one was killed or hurt. It was simply a report on progress, which can seem tragic or hopeful, depending on where you stand. But I couldn't help but feel for these people, more than for the victims of other disasters. I couldn't help imagine the lake slowly spreading like a hemorrhage, in that beautiful, effortless way water does.

I heard Mom shift in her bed. She took a deep breath, followed by a long valley of silence her breathing sometimes falls into. As I waited for the next inhale, I pictured being one of the villagers on top of a mountain there in China overlooking that completed, stillborn lake. It would seem almost natural—how could all that water not? The fishing boats floating across the surface, the trees growing right up to the shore. It would seem almost peaceful—the lapping of the tiny waves against the mountain, the reflection of the giant sky on the water—except for everything I knew existed underneath.

When My Mother Died

When my mother died, Easter was just a few squares away. The day felt like a porcelain basket of fruit, dropped to the ground. A thousand bottles of red wine flowed across the living room floor, and I felt the miscarriage begin, of the child I'd been carrying my entire life. I became someone without knees, living in an abandoned house. When my mother died, it was like witnessing a passenger train derail, the faces from all those legends and cocktail parties smearing past me like rain. A wasp ceased thrashing in the water glass by the sink. And all the colored houses in the neighborhood slipped down into the valley without a whisper of sound. I walked all day and into the night, with shoes that would never fit. Far outside the city, the moon pulled its coat up over its face and left me in an empty field. The earth was so dense, I could not drive a hole into it. I could only stand, like a tree without root, until the wind forced me to the ground.

Sweeping

Here I am sweeping—the hallway, the bedroom, the living room, the porch. I have swept them a hundred times, a thousand times—if not these floors exactly, then others like them—swept them out of anger, and frustration, and sorrow for myself. I have swept to stir up dust, to stir up memories and to clear them out. I've swept out of duty, out of need, because I was asked, or paid, or I told myself I would. I have swept to hold back tears and also to cry uninterrupted. And I have cried from having to sweep, from the drudgery, and simply from the dust. I have swept to clear out the old, to make room for the new, for those who have come and those who have not come, for those who have noticed, those who would never notice, and those who would only notice if I hadn't. I have swept for peace of mind, when I thought that peace of mind could not be found anywhere other than the handle of the broom.

I have swept up nearly nothing, and I have swept a year's worth of dirt, great pillows of dust and skin and hair, leaves and cobwebs and blades of grass. I have swept up thread and buttons and floss, coins and screws and nuts. I've swept up sticks and pebbles, notes and stubs, clasps and lids. I have swept up every color of the rainbow, and many colors not found in a rainbow—indescribable shades of gray and brown which no one ever describes.

I sweep them up and away, as I am doing now, with a brush and a brush and a brush of the broom, the bulk of the dusty cloud ahead of me like some reluctant animal, a portion of it scurrying back to re-dust the floor. I sweep knowing nothing will ever be clean, even for a moment, but still I sweep. I sweep like the women I once saw in Katmandu, out in the early morning, sweeping the dirt roads in front of their houses.

Yes, I once had a life, traveled the world, with nothing pinning me down. But now I am bound to this house—to cleaning and caring for it. But my life is not without purpose. I have simply learned to become like those women sweeping the dirt roads at dawn. Our work is not futile. We sweep each day, that the world may be—not clean exactly, never *clean*—but cleaner. And this is enough.

A Future Story

This story takes place in the future, though not far in the future—just an hour or two from now. You will have finished reading this story when this story takes place. You will be up and about, getting on with your day. The story itself, if it left any impression at all, will begin to fade in your mind as a hundred other things distract you—returning to work, getting something to drink, meeting up with a friend, or figuring out what your next meal will be.

But still, you will be different than the you who is reading this story. Unlike the present you, the you of this story will have already read to the end, will already know what happens. Or maybe the you of this story decided not to finish reading and has that smug satisfaction of putting down a story that was picked up with some hope of entertainment, then concluding it was unworthy of your time.

Or it might be that there are several yous, and as you read this, you come to see that the story is really about the choices you make and don't make, the infinite potential selves created at every moment. If so, the you in the future, the one who wins out over all the other potential yous, is like a victorious gladiator, one who has slain a hundred other ideas and possibilities, pushing you toward one particular point of view. But is that the you you want to be, the most forceful you, the most persuasive? Is that the you you want to be there in the future, a few hours from now?

As you can see, you have some choices to make, serious ones. Perhaps deciding to read this far was not the best choice. You can never unread a story, though you can always choose to read it later, or to never finish reading it. But, since this story is set in the future, it might help you make better decisions—to not read it might let you stumble forward unwisely. Unless knowing how things turn out an hour or so from now makes you overthink what you should do or not do. Oedipus comes to mind, all his efforts to avoid his fate leading to his fate.

Which is to say, you may not have a choice really, in reading this story or not. If you've stopped, then perhaps you were destined to stop. If you're still here on this page, then perhaps that was always your fate. But the you of this story, which takes place after this story ends, already knows all that. A couple hours from now, that you is thinking, *This is me in the future. I am now the character of that story, and I see how this is exactly how the story goes.*

Which is to say, you don't need to read on—you just need to be patient, and in an hour or two, the rest of the story will come to you. It will come to you with a singular, unique ending, which only you will know, because it is your story, and everything you've done and are doing now has made it turn out the way that it has.

Acknowlegments

This collection would not be possible without substantial institutional support from The Virginia Commission of the Arts, The Ucross Foundation, The Eastern Frontier Foundation, and Stockton University.

Special thanks to individuals who gave me feedback on this work, including Amanda Banner, Mary Boyes, Beth Castiglione, Julie Chinitz, Tom DeHaven, Lee Fishman, Laura Holliday, Kath Hubbard, Melanie Lamaga, Kathryn Larson, Jana Llewellyn, Robin Matthews, Lisa Meritz, Patty Smith, Elizabeth Spencer, Jacob Staub, Bill Tester, Martha Turner, Andrew White, and Cass Winner.

Thanks to my great colleagues in the Stockton literature program and to all the lovely people in my Richmond writing group and Philadelphia workshops, from which many of these stories were born or revised.

I deeply appreciate Nickole Brown, who offered valuable edits and ushered this collection into the right hands, and Kevin Watson, for being the right hands.

Many thanks, too, for those who encourage and inspire me, including Per Bjorkman, Barbara Bonadio, Laura Browder, Aneta Dybska, Dominika Ferens, Glyn Hughes, Robert Kokott, Greg LeClair, Triel Lindstrom, Charles and Raasa Leela de Montebello, Diana Puntar, David Thomas, and Sasha Vodnik. I have deep gratitude for my parents, who filled my childhood with stories, and for Courtney Doucette, with whom I've shared so many more.

NATHAN ALLING LONG was born in Washington, D.C., grew up in a log cabin in rural Maryland, and studied literature at the University of Maryland. After graduating, he traveled in Southeast Asia, practiced in a Thai Buddhist monastery, lived on a rural commune in central Tennessee, and co-founded a queer community center in Richmond, Virginia. Between these adventures, Nathan completed an MA in English from Carnegie Mellon and an MFA from Virginia Commonwealth, where he was the first Truman Capote Literary Trust Fellow. He currently lives in Philadelphia and teaches creative writing at Stockton University.

Nathan's work has appeared on *NPR*, in over a dozen anthologies, and in over fifty journals, including *Tin House*, *Glimmer Train*, *Indiana Review*, *The Sun*, and *Crab Orchard Review*. He has been awarded a Mellon Foundation Fellowship, a Virginia Commission of the Arts Grant, work scholarships to Bread Loaf Writers Conference, and three Pushcart Prize nominations. His stories have also won the international 2015 Open Road Review Short Story Prize, the international 2017 OWT Short Fiction Prize, and been finalists in seven *Glimmer Train* short story contests.

For more information, other stories, or essays, please visit http://wp.stockton.edu/longn/

CPSIA information can be obtained
at www.ICGtesting.com
Printed in the USA
LVHW112308120319
610461LV00001B/141/P